FLESH
WOUNDS
AND
PURPLE
FLOWERS

D1565298

FLESH WOUNDS

AND

PURPLE FLOWERS

The Cha-Cha Years

Francisco Ibañez-Carrasco

ARSENAL PULP PRESS
Vancouver

FLESH WOUNDS AND PURPLE FLOWERS
Copyright © 2001 by Francisco Ibañez-Carrasco

ARSENAL PULP PRESS
103-1014 Homer Street
Vancouver, BC
Canada v6b 2w9
arsenalpulp.com

The publisher gratefully acknowledges the support of the Canada Council for
the Arts and the B.C. Arts Council for its publishing program, and the support
of the Government of Canada through the Book Publishing Industry
Development Program for its publishing activities.

Design by Solo
Cover photo used with permission of Rodrigo de los Rios
Printed and bound in Canada

CANADIAN CATALOGUING IN PUBLICATION DATA:
Ibañez-Carrasco, J. Francisco (Jose Fancisco), 1963–
    Flesh wounds and purple flowers

    ISBN 1-55152-098-2

    1. Title.
PS8567.B32F53 2001   C813'.6   C2001-910457-X
PR9199.4.I22F53 2001

I would like to acknowledge
the financial support of the
Multiculturalism Program,
Department of Canadian Heritage
which made possible the
completion of this manuscript.

Many thanks to the people at
Arsenal Pulp Press for their support,
in particular to Brian Lam and Blaine Kyllo.
And many thanks to Beth Easton, Linda Field,
and James Johnstone for giving such thorough
consideration to my writing.

To foes and friends, nurses,
and my mother Isabel,
in sickness and health.
To all the men, *locas*, and queens
I have loved before.

We said it, enraptured,
and believed it perfectly,
that we would all be queens
and would one day reach the sea

– Gabriela Mistral, 1938

THE MORPHINE FLOWS THROUGH MY ARTERIES carrying a thick syrup of visions. *Chispazos de locura y lucidez incendian el tramado hirsuto de mi afiebrada memoria.* Expectant eyes observe me from a distance, scrutinizing my tenuous signals. I wasn't prepared for this. Who is ever prepared? I wish I were at home surrounded by the objects I cherish and nestled by the quiet hum of the refrigerator. Trapped inside this antiseptic, whitewashed display case I flap my wings like a distressed butterfly. I can't dance in here. I dance up a storm down the long and melancholic corridors in the uneasy debris of this evening. A clumsy choreography of garbled words plunges out from my tumescent lips, leaping in capricious pirouettes that chill in mid-air like ice picks, falling to the ground and crashing into a diaspora of crystal tears. Who writes as I speak?

It's Tuesday morning again. I make my way down a street to a *feria* in Santiago dodging the vendors, their carts, their baskets, and their extended hands filled with livestock. The fish, the chicken, and the rabbits let their heavy blue tongues hang out for me with cruel smirks, *una morisqueta cruel.* Their limbs and heads simmer in a *cazuela*, an alchemic stew whose whiff impregnates the air. Skillful hands add corn meal, beans, bulbs, beads, twigs, seeds, clays, stones, harsh wool, threads, fresh green leaves, fruits, aromatic spices, cumin, coriander, and a fickle sting of cracked black pepper. It's the smell found deep in the armpits of males who have worked long hours under the dusty sun, hammering, nailing, forcing, pressing with square fingers, their incensed eyes lusting after fat maids who are out running their daily errands. *Veo a las fámulas meridionales cargando las compras, la fruta y la carne en cambuchos de periódico, embutidas, rozagantes en sus vestidos de percala floreada sin mangas, cargando los niños de la casa patronal entre sus sobacos sudorosos y fuertes, impregnados de perfume barato y con las greñas de pelo sobre la frente, pelo azabache lavado con champú Sinalca y cepillado a tirones.* Women who do the cha-cha down the sinuous sidewalk. The clack-clack of their frenetic *chancletas. Mujeres fuertes como mi madre, esclavas modernas en un país que cambió su economía, su maquillaje, pero se aferró a sus castas sociales. El rock, la cumbia, la salsa, el merengue, el rap, el mambo y el chachacha* collapse in a dissonant fugue, *un vacilón,* punctuated by car horns that pierce the crazy tangerine afternoon. *Por las bambalinas se escapa esta bataclana, la reina del cha-cha-chá, arrebatada como un insecto de incendiario color.* Crooning I go: *Un pasito p'alante, un pasito p'atras.* She wants it real bad.

The urban cacophony quiets down. I hear the muffled noises of nurses, like doves puttering around, worrying over my body, cooing, cooling down this fever. *Ahora huele a menta, a caricia de manzanilla, y agua de rosas, las esencias de la tranquilidad.* Now, it begins to rain. It's the unstable climate of my soul that drenches me in cold sweat. I store in my mind the lines of letters and books, overheard utterances, and the essential lyrics of schmaltzy love songs – "When I was young I listened to the radio / waiting for my favorite song. . . ." Hello, good day. Whoever you are, who has come to my bedside, to this humid shore, to my pillow of rustling memories, someone who listens gently to the slow tide of my respiration, a nursemaid for my memories, please, do hold these fibers with the tip of your fingers, the threads of an invisible cord instrument, thread them and you will touch a material that feels like my most intimate lining – "When they get to the part that he's breaking her heart / they can even make me cry / just like before / it's yesterday once more." Poor Karen, she died so young, and so thin, so seductive is consumption, so horrifying the deterioration of our edifices, but a strict diet of saturated life is only a modest requirement to be forever put in safekeeping in the memories of everyone.

The dance, *el vaivén de la danza*, the flesh, the fresh, the food, the puzzling love of men. Living has pleased me much. I never lost faith. *Mi amor, señor, tu que dijiste, mi paz os dejo, mi paz os doy. No mires nuestros pecados sino la fé de esta loca.* Rednecks, loonies, intellectuals, soldiers, preachers, peasants, cops, carpenters, teachers, cousins, politicians, men who worked with their muscles, with their teeth, with their feet, with a few words, with quills and paper, men who traveled the body I extended before them like a road, inscribed their words on my tongue, mapping their conversions and recantations. They claimed ownership over me, a river torrent overcome, a mountain peak conquered, a battle hard won. Branded like property, fondled like a new car, an appliance, a credit card; scolded as if I were their offspring, their wife or their subaltern; revered like a little statuette in an altar, a superstition that must be concealed and secretly practiced. I didn't live in their houses, but in many ways, I governed their intimacy with rules carefully engraved in the small back of my neck, placed upon my palms. Paid like a whore and adored like a virgin, I offered myself with a faith that I wore around my neck like an *escapulario*. *Negros, chinos, gringos, cholos, morenos, ladinos* and *indios* who stepped through my open door to occupy, conquer, and reform me, discovered, much to their surprise, that I was resilient and free.

I remember the last afternoon class on Thursdays. It was physical education. My classmates would mock me.

"Sissy, you sissy, come and touch the big one." Lewd remarks addressed to me. Little they knew.

"*M'hijita,* come and sit on this!" I became addicted to their braggadocio, their size, their skill, and their locker room stories of indefatigable prowess.

"*A ver si eres tan macho,*" I sneered. "Give it a try, honey." They would go away laughing, wrestling with each other, building up a desire that later, in the back of the schoolyard, would be deployed on me. As silence fell upon the soccer courts and the shower stalls, no more stomping and yelling; only the unnerving sound of a few drops, leaks, echoes; he, the teacher, a stocky man in his forties, who said he could have been a track and field star, was always there to inflict his frustrations on my skin. In a corner of the gym, I would once more become victim and victor. Ah! The sweet right of males to do whatever they fucking please. *Dios bendiga al hombre hecho – y derecho – a su imagen y semejanza.* God teaches us to kiss the hand that feeds us – *a poner la otra mejilla.*

A yarn spins and twists, its friction causes abrasions that cause the skin of the dreamweaver to bleed; not all ends well. My early romances were garments of tenuous manufacture that my lovers could not see; they could only hasten to tear the veils apart to get to the young flesh. Every time I retained a keepsake, a valuable spell to conjure up the power of the queen – *la loca* – the crazed effeminate, the weak one. I learned the art of seducing *machos* by sweetly kissing their Achilles' heels. Ah, the sports coach is but one delicious example, his precious private moments, the scent of his arms, the scent of his fear if I were to "casually" run into him the next day, surrounded by jocks, fear flowed like the scent of a poison, barely contained, hidden away, yet at times so intense that it would bleed through the scared apples of his eyes. Night after night for many of my young years, in the tensed cordage of slender male muscles, I incited a rhythm that started like a hesitant cadence, *un vaivén,* and wound up as an unrestrained cha-cha. I heard the inflections of their rusty voices, unshaven, wet thick lips asking me questions, formulating threats, making counterfeit promises. *Este es el cuerpo del hombre, dichosos los llamados a esta cena.*

Every story seemed the first, every romance supreme; every night seemed like the Last Supper, our cups flooded with sweat and tears. I memorized this song when I was learning English: "You and I will make each night the first / every day a beginning / spirits rise and the dance is unrehearsed." Sing, Barbra, sing! I acted out its lyrics as I made a pilgrimage to the shrine of a body to consummate my prayers, make my ablutions, touch it with devotion to request a miracle from its Lord. His breath was the Holy Spirit, his flesh was bread, his blood wine. *Señor no soy digno de que entres en mi cuerpo pero una palabra tuya bastará para sanarme.* One commits the greatest sin of losing oneself for the lofty end of giving oneself up to a man.

Mourners and women labour over quilts and knitting, *las arpilleras,* stitch by stitch, *hilvanar y zurcir,* they piece together the seconds into a seamless desperation. I stitched together an icon with threads of descriptions found in newspapers, women's magazines, songs, and letters describing secret wishes. I infused him with imagination, with the tenderness and love of nuns, sisters, virgins, whores, and housewives. *Purifica mis labios, del pecado, de la sal, de la saliva ardiendo en lenguas de fuego, purifica estos labios para anunciar tu evangelio.* I stood by my man even when he was a cross to bear, even when he crossed me. I needed the kindness and the impiety of strangers, the texture of their bodies, their bullying roughness, and their foolishness to make me the reigning queen of a heart scratched wide open with a raging, long nail, letting out a hysterical streak of jungle red blood. *Esta es mi sangre dichosos los llamados a esta cena.* Once my blood vessels had dried up to engorge each one of his, I would turn to him and say, "Take me." A growl that would come up from the depths. "Pay me back."

Maybe it is true that we only live once, once within an entire lifetime that is. We only bloom once. I wish I could have lived over a long period of time much of what was tightly packed into barely a decade so I could savour it. It's not that I didn't enjoy it; it's only that it was so quick, like lightning. One strike and you're out, *gringos* say – or is it three? The virus was one, the ignition, the catalyst, the inspiration, and the mermaid's song that never ceased. Nothing after that followed the course described in sentimental memoirs. The migration was the second, the foreignness of the tongue, and the bitter aftertaste of the everyday. Being queer, a member of that well-tolerated and highly neurotic bunch, was the third strike; three strikes and you're out, not out of the game, but out *there*, exposed.

Tonight, I feel the urge to summon the presence of all these men wherever they may be. Like the many nights when the fevers of desire or loneliness caught up with me and I ran to the dark streets to throw myself in the arms of the first man who crossed my way, as its name deliciously indicates it – *la loca*, the madwoman. *¡Que canten todos los maricones como las sirenas para atraer a los hombres!* At the edge of ecstasy or eclipse, there is always one more man, to save the day, and not write it off as a bad cheque. Looking good, as always, my sweet idol, looking good: fiery eyes, sturdy torso, thick hands, your crotch growing like my appetite, *una promesa de operático final, de gran crimen o suicidio pasional, de gran coger y expirar.* Let's dance, slowly . . . clasped around your solid legs, standing in the stormy way of your breathing. Your lies seduce my heart and the night deceives the sun and goes on forever. *¡Baila el merengue, mi vida, como si estuvieras cogiendo!* Tonight I'll be kissed goodbye by sailors, by fathers I will be kissed good-night, by brothers and lovers I will be incestuously touched. Tonight I'll be surrounded by compassionate sisters who softly blow to melt the blue ice that vitrifies my body. In the screen of my mind a million flashes, fresh cuts of lovely purple flowers, explode centre stage, *como luces de bengala, como un pirómano en mi corazón, ¡Baila!* "Last dance/this is our last chance/for romance/tonight. . . ." Tonight, I dance away in a ballroom festooned by starfish, a jungle of intravenous catheters, hoses and strands, purple flowers, viruses, and bacteria. You Tarzan, me, Jane, and would Jane like to dance in my arms? – one by one each one of my surprising gentleman suitors extends a gentle hand to invite me to dance, and we twirl on a mother-of-pearl dance floor surrounded by the shrieks of restless birds – the infusion machine stops and complains with loud beeps. Someone comes and hangs another bag of a purple potion, the bottled-up delay, the trickling pain of my friends, my soul sisters, more than next of kin, more than victims or oppressed minorities. I'll drink to that!

IN 1986, AFTER SPENDING SEVERAL MONTHS IN Cuba, Camilo had problems getting off the island via Mexico City because he held a Chilean passport and Mexicans had no diplomatic relations with Chile at that time. The stern diplomatic employee explained that they had let Camilo into the island via Mexico, but they refused to let him out the same way after he had twice delayed his departure. It is probable that even if the Mexicans had not had any diplomatic problems with Camilo's holding a Chilean passport, Camilo himself would have started an international incident; such was his desire to delay his sojourn as much as possible. Kirsten and Dave had gotten off the island a few weeks earlier and had left Camilo with the rest of their money – which was not much at all – and their few remaining toiletries, which were valuable possessions given the permanent scarcity of luxury items. It was only during their last days in Havana that Camilo had established a strong bond with Kirsten and had confessed to her his determined love for Leandro, the black poet trapped working at a communist printing press, in a barren marriage with a party officer's daughter, and in a crumbling apartment in *La Habana Vieja*. Kirsten truly understood and she reciprocated by telling his new confidant that she, herself, had fallen for the unreserved charms of the islanders and that, although she had to leave, she would be soon severing her ties with Dave. Cuba had given her a different perspective and she was returning to Canada to do something very different and – as she called it – very "real."

Although Camilo sabotaged his own departure several times by not trying to find a way out, by missing appointments with Mexican and Cuban authorities, and by paying a small fortune to reschedule his flights, the time came that he could not sustain this precarious situation any longer. In a garbled collect call to Andrew and Sol in Vancouver, Camilo pleaded for a personal loan and promised he would pay them as soon as he returned and got employment back in Canada. Finally, once the season of rains had started, the U.S. *Sección de Interéses* agree to extend Camilo a visa to enter the States. Minutes after the sun had plunged into a humid sunset, Camilo boarded a plane that connected the pitch dark of *La Habana* with the bejeweled coast of Florida in about forty-five minutes. His heart had shrunk during that final night that he and his lover had spent in each other's arms. In Miami, a world of drive-ins, overfed *maquiladoras* by day, clothed in Armani by night, and banana republic expatriates, unbearable under the heavy-handed and muggy summer, Camilo saw Leandro's face in each passer-by, in each stranger, and his heart seemed to stop and turn every time he heard a low, inviting voice nearby, only to find that it was a mirage. He stayed with Mariana Nomeolvides, a conspicuously well-off Chilean woman anchored, teeth and nails, in a garishly furnished apartment in the heart of Coral Gables. A couple of weeks after his arrival, Camilo, who had been crying since the day he touched down in Miami, caught a Greyhound to Manhattan.

 IF I COULDN'T STAY IN CUBA, I FELT I NEEDED TO travel as far as possible from it quickly, without turning my head. These were my thoughts as I was leaving Miami to visit Cesar in Manhattan. A change of unclear magnitude, some kind of change, had occurred to me on that island, in the arms of Leandro, under the consistent weight of his body, and in the small and fleeting day to day that I had created there. In the end, it was all illusory and short-lived, but it made me understand that this would be the nature of things in life, always moving on, trying hard to keep a few underpinnings to a borrowed reality. However, the island was also healing, the many poems that Leandro had trickled in my ears to make me dizzy with want had reminded me of things past, after my many years in Vancouver. Hearing and speaking Spanish again was like healing a wound by exposing it to those fresh elements: Leandro's words, the skin singed by the sun, the agitated everyday life.

Perched on an uncomfortable Greyhound seat, trekking up the East Coast to New York, I tried to put together the events that had so serendipitously led me to Cuba. Although my first reaction was to sensibly use the money I had saved waiting on tables, cleaning houses, and babysitting to go back to Chile, I chose to go to Cuba – can't tell why. Perhaps it was the same intuition that had made me stay in Vancouver in the first place instead of following my friends' paths and remaining in the promised land of New York. Perhaps it was because growing up in Chile I had only heard from rich people, the media, and the priests how horrible Cubans and their communism were. I had also heard in *sotto voce* how important and wonderful the revolution was from my mother's poor communist friends and from my political activist classmates at the university in Santiago. In Canada, it was a different story.

Cuba was exalted by naïve long-distance revolutionaries who were fed from the memories of the many exiled *Latinos* living a life of thick nostalgia and resentment. When I heard that two of Andrew's university classmates were planning a backpacking trip to the country that for Chileans was the epitome of *déclassé* vulgarity and populist dictatorship – the boogieman of each Latin American stiff upper lip – I had to go, so I met Kirsten and Dave – who looked fairly reluctant and guarded, not unusual for Anglo people, I thought – and convinced them that the three of us could travel together. These two were a pair of earthy Birkenstock granola *gringos* who wanted to go to the island to learn the main precepts of socialism, the real thing, in what they called their "ideological cradle."

It was established that Cuba was like a magnet for political ingénues like us. But, it had a particular attraction for me, I felt, as the offspring of a right wing dictatorship, born and raised in forced ignorance in a masquerade of order and dignity. I knew there had to be something there that had both electrified and terrified all *Chilenos* when Salvador Allende was elected in 1970. Isn't it ironic that I had to go to Cuba to understand the jungle of whispers, veiled gestures, and silences in which I grew up? Cesar and Italo thought that the whole thing was ridiculous, only my clever design to get me some "black meat." Anyway, after a couple of months of preparation, I joined Kirsten and Dave. Their idea of traveling was backpacking and eating twelve-grain bread and fresh squeezed orange juice. Fortunately, we found out that backpackers weren't welcome on the island; we would have to stay in a small *pension* in *La Habana*. I liked Kirsten better, she had a knack for listening to stories and writing them down, said she wanted to be an ethnographer, whatever that was, and she was always ready to sit down and listen. Dave was a bore, an anal retentive, pale textbook Marxist, one of those *gringos* who had "a plan" to get ahead and be managing Canadian international development projects in one of those goody-two-shoes non-profit

Ottawa organizations that hold agonizing hands with the third world, he said he would be doing this in about six to eight years, and I am sure this is what he came to do – I didn't follow his tracks.

My thoughts dissipated as the bus made its slow entrance into the Big Apple and I could see the path I had left closing behind me, it would be a long time before I could retrace my steps back to the island, but I knew this is the way life is, one is born to pass, and passing is all there is. I grew up listening to Joan Manuel Serrat vocalizing Antonio Machado's verses – *"todo pasa y todo queda, pero lo nuestro es pasar, pasar haciendo caminos, caminos sobre la mar."* My passing through the island left but a tenuous wake over the seas after I left Leandro in Havana. The thing is, I couldn't stomach Miami for too long – it's so fucking plastic – this is why I went to New York, to the Bronx, to Cesar's, my close friend since high school, and to make some money to get back to Vancouver by working under the table. Little I knew of what awaited me on this new island.

New York was an unexpected world, ablaze, viscous like a slow penetration. I stepped off the Greyhound at the Port Authority, looking like Evita before taking the first bite of the Big Apple. And when I did, the city's strange flavours began percolating through me like a powerful new drug, they came up through the pavement like salt rejected by the earth, curdling in the midday hour; abrupt impressions jabbing my eyes, calling my senses, demanding twenty-four hours of avid attention, the city that never sleeps. A rotating kaleidoscope of grooves and vibrations, *colores incendiarios,* loud boom boxes, *caricias pastosas,* arson, *los celos,* jealousy, *y el verano impregnado en mi piel.* During the sensuous cruelty of the afternoons when I was off work, I found solace in the fire hydrants burst open. Children and adults scattered around the gush of water – *en tremendo jaleo* – splashing, laughing, and squealing like birds. The smell of frying meat, the stench of urine, the intoxicating body odour all made me high and carried me deep into the evenings. The extreme temperatures constantly collided in my body. Coming into a building, the air conditioning would feel like freezing whiplash, and stepping out, the hot humidity would slowly marinate me. I spent hours meandering the city, drenched, or sitting on the black and white tiled floor by the entranceway, watching the fat *Nuyorican* brown women fan themselves, sluggishly walking their humanity, *con ese devaneo sabrosón*, galvanizing the gluttony in the devouring eyes of men. *Cuando calienta el sol aqui en la playa, siento tu cuerpo vibrar cerca de mi.* I had to get out to Manhattan and get me some. Sex was the only free thing in the city. In the receding heat of dark alleys, corridors, or basements, wrapped in a hazy web of sensations, I met other bodies. Like a hummingbird, I fluttered into the shadows drawing the fluids expressed by strange fruits.

Once the last shred of autumn rolled over, I had to leave. None of the hands that touched me in New York could abrade the smell of Leandro, the mix of tenderness and bravery pressed against my skin. Yet I had to move even farther away like Machado had predicted: "All things die and all things live forever; but our task is to die, to die making roads, roads over the sea." It is as if Machado had predicted what would happen to me, to us, down the road.

CAMILO FELL PREY TO THE BURNING SPELL OF *La Habana* and its noisy and ripe midday hours. Speaking Spanish was a rediscovered thrill. The nearness of other bodies was startling. His Canadian training in bylaws, policies, and regulations initially made him shy and prevented him from touching, it was harassment, invasion of personal space. Camilo, Kirsten, and Dave stayed at a small pension in *El Vedado* close to the university. Their host was a retired high-ranking soldier who gave them long speeches about *la revolución* that made the eyes of the *gringos* sparkle with inspiration. The first weeks Camilo sat around with them listening to the endless chatter of the old man about *antifidelistas* and *el enemigo yanqui*, over heaping plates of *moros y cristianos,* fried *malanga* and *cerdo* that Kirsten and Dave, staunch vegetarians in Vancouver, ate without uttering a single complaint. Other days they dragged Camilo with them and engaged in moral dilemmas about post-colonialism and cultural imperialism with students at the *Universidad de la Habana.* Camilo made himself a mental promise to go back to university one of these days to learn their pompous jargon. Camilo was stuck with them, playing their jungle guide and interpreter. This situation, he realized, would not allow him to find out whether any of those earnest political science university students could think about anything other than Marxism. Nonetheless, some of their stares lingered on, over the Marxist tracts, in a comradely embrace a tad too tight.

Although Camilo initially got distracted by Kirsten and Dave's earnest political agenda to learn about *La Revolución*, before long he figured his way around how to sneak out and how to illegally exchange *fulas* for *pesos*, something that his prudish fellow travelers had made him swear he would not do, something in which every other Cuban seemed glad to engage. He began to wriggle his tail around town like a lizard under the sweltering sun. He basked in the attention. He did not mind being an *extranjero* there. It was unlike being a foreigner in Canada. His casual attitude and his foreign Spanish accent opened the doors to many people and many homes. Cuban men and women alike returned his flirtations and the smiles he put on constantly, like a child showing off a new outfit.

He would get lost in the labyrinth of *La Habana Vieja* and strike up conversations that turned into long-drawn-out evenings, drinking cold beer, sitting languidly in the shade, smiling, listening, catching the whiffs of tobacco breath from men, yearning for a thick caress that would gently push him against the refreshing stucco wall of a *solar*. However, Camilo's diplomatic relations invariably wound up in a request to visit the nearest *turistienda*, for tourists only, armed with a smuggled roll of American dollars that someone had saved and a shopping list. Every man he met had a string of relatives; down the street, every person was a *prima*, *tio,* or *cuñado* who needed something from the *turistienda*. With a degree of jealousy, Camilo sat in public spaces and verandas during those first weeks, looking at the Cuban men coyly taking their *queridas*, their *novias*, and their *madres* with smiles, squinting eyes, and wide gestures, like dancers getting ready to rehearse, complimenting each other's hair and each other's appearance, slowly setting the stage for the dimming of the sunlight and the dance that would ensue later.

ON A SULTRY SATURDAY NIGHT, UNDER A PEACEFUL green roof of *Framboyanes, Ceibos, Almendros,* and *Tamarindos* I saw Leandro for the first time. *¡Un morenazo! Cargando pesados músculos como un arbol.* Tall like those trees, slender, solid. I swallowed hard several times and my saliva thickened into something like syrup. I was at a free concert in *Pabellón Cuba* in *Calle 23*; it was crowded, loud, and festive. He was well-flanked by a petite black woman with a bandana that strangled a mane of wild curls, and surrounded by friends, laughing, savouring ice cream, talking, and I saw his eyes chasing after mine repeatedly. I left, I came back, I left again, went around the block, came back again, and the band played long sets of jazz into the evening, making the bodies swing to the rhythm. Finally, I simply sat there, mesmerized, unable to take my eyes off his movements and his smile. After a long preamble, a drum roll in my heart, the woman who embraced him walked purposefully over to where I was and talked to me. She asked me to approach her husband (her husband!) discreetly because he wanted to ask me a favour and there were too many cops around. I got it; I was in for another excursion to a *turistienda.* I said nothing and followed her to one of the side entrances and then into a dark back street. Her man was there, smoking, leaning against the rusty iron railing of an old house, sheltered in the dark. The young woman kissed him and took her leave. I can't remember his first words, something about the music, uttered softly, cajoling, and his long fingers were moving in the air near me. He slightly arched his left eyebrow, closing in on me.

"*¿Como tu te llamas?*"

"*Camilo.*"

"*¿De adonde tu eres?*"

"*Chile . . . er, bueno ahora de Canadá.*"

"*¿Andas solo?*"

"¡Si, si!"

"¿Solo? ¿No tienes miedo?" Fear? It never entered my mind. I shrugged. He stepped closer. *"Con tanto zingado maricón que anda por ahi, y tu tan bonito."* One of his ample palms landed on my shoulder, at the back of my neck, a light squeeze that gave me a jolt. The evening tightened around my eyes. Suddenly, I could not make sense. I felt like a bleached blonde, a perky *gringa* in a stupid infomercial, not my most glamorous personality. He asked me if I could get some American cigarettes at the *turistienda* and my feelings crash landed, but I had become a bit quicker on the uptake. Why envy their *queridas, novias,* and *madres* any longer when I could play *la turista.*

"Ah, yeah, and what do I get in return?" I laid it on thick, or so I thought. Instead of backing up, he smoothly placed his thick lips upon mine and slid his tongue in between for what seemed like an eternity. He stopped and laughed, knowing that he had called my bluff.

"How old are you exactly?" I mustered in my most mature tone.

"Old enough to take on something like you – come, we'll take a detour to the *turistienda*, at the *Nacional* they close at eight." Incited by his insolence, disarmed by the aftertaste in my mouth, I followed. We arrived at the hotel through a couple of dark streets to avoid the harassment of policemen who tried to discourage *jineteras* and *jineteros* from picking up greasy Italian and Spanish men who wore tacky, thick golden rings and lecherous smiles. Like many times before I got a stash of dollars to purchase cigarettes and export Baccardi rum, dutifully ran my errand, and met him two blocks down the road; I had only purchased the cigarettes.

"They didn't have the rum you wanted, I will have to come back tomorrow." He smiled incredulously.

And then I asked, "What do I get in return – if I come back?"

"You get to be mine tonight."

"What about her – your wife?"

"She gets her fair share." His hand guided mine skillfully so I could assess the enormity of this statement.

I went back to the hotel and got the booze and we sat taking big gulps at the far end of the *malecón*, watching the light of the moon skinny-dip into the waters, then we walked the poorly lit streets for hours, *la vereda tropical*, his words, *como un susurro calladito*, weaving my fantasies into thick flames that spiraled up into the dark sky – *lenguas de fuego al revés clavandose en el cielo*. There was no more rushing of seconds, no clicking, no tick-tock, we walked slowly up the *Calle* G and sat for a long time by the curb of a winding street plagued with languid willow trees. Curious eyes passing in the night would notice us and walk on by, accomplices out looking for satisfaction themselves. The morning light soon brushed across the quiet streets, casting long-legged shadows. Then we headed to the narrow streets of *Centro Habana*, past the empty windows of fancy yesteryear department stores inhabited by ghosts, startled by the playful putt-putt of old Fords.

It was almost seven in the morning – the sun had already blanched the limpid sky – when we arrived in a gorgeous yet dilapidated 1940s walk-up where Leandro lived. His wife worked days in a factory outside Havana, Leandro worked nights in a printing shop that churned out endless and boring political pamphlets and the occasional poetry booklet. In this tiny apartment, every room was buttressed with thick wooden studs in each corner to delay the defiant erosion of decades of Cuban revolution. The place looked like a shrine to America, cheap plastic knick-knacks everywhere, things sporting brand names and English words. Leandro took me to the roof and showed me how the buildings in *Centro Habana*, like sand castles, crumble a little every day, sometimes one room at a time, forcing people out of their homes. With a long finger, he pointed at all these things and at the horizon where he, and every young Cuban, he said, wanted to go. Then he pointed at the hardest structure of all that – he assured me – defied all laws of gravity and buttressed his corner of the world. He led me back into his apartment.

Inside, sheltered from the heat, dazzled by the sun, I discovered that one's memory is frail, that no matter how much one thinks one has lived, there is always erosion and abandon, that experience is a majestic building that crumbles a tiny bit each day and needs to be renovated constantly. I discovered that I knew nothing and that in Leandro's arms I knew little or nothing again. My ankles were firmly locked in the grip of his two thick hands and the pain of his slow penetration was tempered by a drip of sweet words from his lips, like notes and cues given to initiate a choreography, a dance that wasn't stilted or rushed, a dance unlike the Canadian athletic sexual games or the hurried and timorous sexual dance of Chileans. It always started *cadencioso* like a *bolero* – "*Tu me acostumbraste a todas esas cosas / y tu me enseñaste, que son maravillosas. / Sutil, llegaste a mi como la tentación*" – that found its delectable way through the limbs and gradually turned into a frenzy. "*Goza, coño, goza,*" Leandro potently commanded from above, like a Caribbean dragon, a loud spitting animal, hissing, outfitted with *sonajas* and *cascabeles*, like one in a carnival; it opened its fangs, huffing, laughing wide, to swallow them in a baptism of fire in its guts, the innards of the city, ablaze, *incandescente, incendiando el mediodia,* fastened by their legs and fingers, biting, like insects, *alacránes,* embroiled in a ferocious fight – "*Dejate, suavecito, un pasito p'alante, otra p'atras. Y ahora mas rápido, así, mas rápido hasta que sea un chachachá, hasta que coga candela el alma y duela sabroso*" – in this way he seduced me, my Leandro, a consummate dancer, as he turned the radio way up, to drown our moans in a cornucopia of *sones, salsas, danzones, mambos,* and *merenges;* our moans that often overflowed through the window and cascaded down the weakened brick walls, washing away the faded stucco. If one of the frequent electrical blackouts suddenly caught us in the midst of crazy making, the radio suddenly muted, we were fully exposed, we would take a brief pause in our agitation to catch our breath, to contort and realign the spine, to bury many promises in each other's necks, and then, we would recklessly resume our labour.

"*Así, papi, así, como me gusta así.*"

"*Dímelo en inglés.*"

"I like it like that, papi, gimme some more." Echoes in the afternoon that tumbled down the stairs like a bouncing ball down to the *solar* where boisterous children played loudly. We could not get enough for days and weeks, always in the midday blaze; our euphoria knew no limits. If someone came knocking at the front door, we would suspend the passion for a moment, panting, almost suffocated – maybe the neighbours chose to believe it was the recently married couple on the third floor making children, or Xiomara's abusive husband letting her have it, chasing her, making her cry – the hell with them, there wasn't enough skin or time to stretch in the hours of the day, there weren't enough fluids to drench, there wasn't enough music and pain seeping through those dilapidated walls.

"*Así, papi, así, me gusta así.*"

"*Goza coño, goza mi azuquitar.*"

The first month in New York I was so in love with Leandro I kept myself chaste for him. I thought of doing that for as long as it would take me to go back to Cuba. I had promised. Cesar, moreover, would sometimes exhibit fastidious hangovers of Chilean sensibility, a collection of bottled-up farts and burps and what-others-might-say and that-is-indecent or worse, low-class. But I wasn't shackled by those silly conventions any more. This was the New York of my disco-bunny dreams, the epicenter of western homosexuality, Greenwich, the piers, the leather bars on Chelsea, and I wanted to wallow in it so bad. Cesar lived in the Bronx, on Rosedale Avenue by St. Lawrence Street where you could get mugged for a couple of bucks and that summer the Molina's convenience store across the building got sprayed twice by drive-by shooters. No weapon was more useful, no instrument more efficient, than my body and its desire. Chastity didn't last long.

Maybe it was the second month there when, on one of my late evening excursions, I pulled a man out from the Adonis theatre where the projection was scratchy and the seats were leathery and slippery. Sonny, the jazz singer, looked like Leandro: tall, big, strong – that was the initial lure – but being American, he had that arrogant and whiny streak in him. Don't know how, but we struck a utilitarian deal. I played the Ike-like top: butch, violent asshole, and he took the Tina role. I wanted to remember and Sonny needed to sing in more ways than one. Often I would go and see him play in the smoky bar down in Greenwich where he sang old American standards. He would blow kisses across the floor and send me one drink after the other. Invariably we would end up listening to Nina Simone and Billie Holliday and having sloppy inebriated sex in the early morning in his apartment in Brooklyn. Sonny would get me in a mood; he had a knack for doing that. I'd put on a macho act and rough him up. It wasn't over till the big queen sobbed. I didn't like to do it. It felt wrong. Next evening he would be up there, behind the mike, crooning again: *I don't know why I should / he isn't good / he beats me too / what can I do? / Oh my man, I love him so.* If anything, I learned to love jazz. Only a lonely encounter much later would explain why Sonny had behaved this way. Some explanations come too late.

CAMILO SPENT A LOT OF TIME WITH CESAR, WHO, despite his sullen and prudish demeanor and frequent grunting, had nothing but support for him. He also spent a lot of time with Juan, who would come around in the afternoons to chat. Juan was in his early forties, although he would never admit to that; a loud queen in their private conversation, he could behave like the toughest dude out on the street. He used to say, "The attitude, I got from *Boricuas*. Fucking good, I learned from Cubans. The sleaze I learned from *gringos*." Camilo was all ears. Juan was frank and streetwise. Coincidentally, Camilo and Juan had been trained as teachers at the same university in Santiago. Juan had left Chile as a result of a witch-hunt when he was a young teacher in a Chilean high school. One, two, or more of his students, this wasn't clear, had accused him of getting them between the sheets, or behind the classroom door – that wasn't clear either. Juan claimed that it was the students who had taken turns seducing him. "Make no mistake, *lola*, the student seduces the teacher, the woman commands over the house and the bed, in brief, whoever is at the bottom is surely in control," he used to say. Then he explained that when he naïvely decided not to keep two-timing his two or three young student lovers, one of them got jealous and told the school principal, a closeted old queen who immediately got him fired and went to the Ministry of Education to try and get his teaching license revoked. That is when Juan, fed up, cornered, had come to New York on lots of borrowed money. Once there, he washed dishes, cleaned washrooms, sold frankfurters at subway stops, shoplifted at Alexander's and, in rough weeks, he had collected cans from garbage bins at Coney Island to exchange for a few coins. He used to save each penny to see Grace Jones at The Saint, or sneak into Studio 54 on weekends. Regularly, he wrote glamorous letters to his lonely mother in Chile, telling her, "If I make it there, I'll make it anywhere,

it's up to you New York, New York," and other song lyrics in transla-
tion. He always enclosed a money order. After a few years, cunning as
he was, Juan saw a trend in people talking dirty on the phone and
established one of the first gay fantasy phone lines in New York, a true
pioneer. That was Juan's big break. From then on, he developed an
incredible repertoire of voices, inflexions, characters, and scenes worthy of any Broadway stage. His reputation extended quickly among
gay *Latinos* and he often gave a helping hand to many a Chilean illegal émigré in Manhattan. This is how he had met Cesar when he had
recently arrived. They struck a complicated but solid friendship and
when times were hard Cesar stayed in Juan's crash-pad-cum-business
office in the Bronx. By the time Camilo went to New York, the
phone line business was thriving and Juan's lover – a gentle and generous old leather man – was the manager, having been lured himself
by Juan's fabulous scenarios. They lived together in a spacious one-
bedroom on 72nd that Camilo loved to visit.

   "My voice is my livelihood," Juan often stated judiciously. "When
I branched out and started making outcalls, I made sure I charged
extra for deep-throating. No one, hear me good, *lola*, no one but
daddy and his Prince Albert get to scratch these vocal chords for free,
they are worth gold!"

At the end of the summer, Camilo went back to Vancouver and stayed
in an old house on Victoria Drive shared by Sol, her little son Esteban,
Andrew, and his lover Garth. Both men had moved to Vancouver two
years earlier to attend the local university. Garth would soon finish his
degree in criminology and his career seemed to occupy a lot of his
thoughts. Sol had recently come to Canada to become the barefoot
and pregnant wife of a logger, a harsh man of sturdy bones and square
jaw lines, about whom she volunteered no further information. Sol
ended up dumping him, going to film school to become an exotic
star in the local highbrow, albeit narrow, Vancouverite firmament.

Camilo had met her at a benefit function for *exiliados* and *desapareci-dos*. They instantly hit if off, establishing quickly that that they were both dutifully listening to the earnest political dribble and ugly poetry of expatriates, primarily to partake in the free wine and cheese. Camilo confided to her that he was staying at the local YMCA, looking for a job, and not having much luck with that or even much to eat. He had seen the poster announcing the somber event and decided to attend. Sol said she was bored and was looking for stout *Latino* characters for her next short film. In the course of that evening, they shared their fortunes and misfortunes and their puzzlement about living in Vancouver. In whispered asides, they also politely admitted a veiled disdain for what they saw as the mediocrity of many of their compatriots. Sol said that Central Americans often shared the provincialism of many Anglo Canadians and Camilo agreed by stating that he found it surprising that Chileans would have far more in common with Anglos than with Caribbeans or Central Americans, and that not in vain were Chileans known as the English of South America. And, by agreeing on a few precarious generalizations, they found a common ground. It also turned out in their animated chat that they had acquaintances in common, Garth and Andrew, and that Sol and little Esteban had started to room with them only a few months ago. Sol assured Camilo that they were very easygoing – at least Andrew was – and would accommodate him for a while. It was thus established that it all was clearly written in the stars. Sol did not even bother to notify her roommates that Camilo would be crashing there for a few weeks. On Sunday morning, the two stalwart men woke up with their habitual hangovers, raging hard-ons, and a peaceful sleeping young queen sprawled on the living room futon.

IT TOOK ME A FEW DAYS TO GET OVER MY INITIAL shock. Vancouver seemed drab, slow, and silent, mired in an insistent drizzle. When my mind got clearer and my eyes shone again the people around me seemed to come back from the grey area I had exiled them to while I was away. For the first time after my long trip, what I had intimately envisioned as a definitive getaway, I realized that I was linked to Vancouver by an umbilical cord that was more than the basic need to live decently or make money. I could have stayed in Cuba – Leandro was now farther than ever and his absence in my body ached like a ghostly pain – maybe I could have stayed in New York, immersed in its fascinating high-strung life, making loads of money under the table like my friends were, certainly more money than I would ever make in Canada. I could have gone to Chile – I promised myself that would be my next destination – I could have done some things differently, yet many roads and my trustworthy intuition had led me back to Vancouver. The word "compromise" weighed heavily on my heart.

Garth and Andrew I knew. I had briefly made their acquaintance before I went to Cuba; they were now living as a couple and they seemed happy to see me again after almost a year. That made me feel good. You can't tell with *gringos*, especially West Coasters, who often seem guarded, distant, and almost indifferent. They can hold back love and attention for a long time and then one fine day, out of the blue, they swing open the door to their hearts. Now, they invite you – come in, now I'm ready. It seemed to me that it would be that way with Andrew, that he would finally give in and get closer, I somewhat craved this, however it seemed that Garth would be an exception to my assumption, he was impenetrable. Soon after I moved in, he finished his university education, and pretty self-righteous about it, I might add, and immediately got himself a job as a welfare cop in the local social assistance office where, by Andrew's account, he was very stern. It was odd, in the evenings when Garth got home, he'd light up a joint and metamorphose into a taciturn and apprehensive being – he'd follow Andrew from room to room like a miserable pet – he'd be jealous of Andrew's time and friendliness with others, particularly the times he spent with Sol, and later with me. I couldn't understand what Andrew saw in him; Garth was almost like a life project of his. He had tenaciously courted him since they had met in a Canada World Youth exchange in Colombia, they were both in their teens – that's where they had met Sol, too. I reckon I was deeply intrigued by Garth's full beard, his deep blue eyes, his rugged countenance that revealed nothing, not even when I had paraded naked in front of him; Teflon men who are able to resist my skillful advances have the effect of egging me on! Certainly that hadn't been the case with Andrew, who on one occasion had fallen prey to my advances in what would have been an explosive experience, had it not been for the strange look on Garth's face, his inability to join us – he had a boner, what more motivation does one need, for goodness' sake! – and the tinge of confusion in his furrowed eyebrows as he stared from the other side of the room, suspended in a cloud of smoke. I guess we were all meant to be friends and friends don't have sex with each other. I had also learned by then that Anglo gay men in British Columbia, those who are out and "proud," require great doses of either drugs or reassurance and what they euphemistically call "safety" to engage in wild and messy sex. Much later, I would learn that there are plenty of *gringos* like that, one has to show them a sign that says "applause" and they do, a sign that says "time to fuck" and they do. As far as the many other gorgeous men that populate the land, well, I didn't even bother looking at Asians or East Indians, Romanians or "my people" as some would refer to them, in general they seemed out of reach and kind of trapped in their own struggles to be themselves and not be shunned by their families – the so-called "communities." Later, I also learned that Garth was a unfaltering "bottom" – *pasiva como figura de porcelana* – as we say in Chile, like a China doll, or worse, like a Raggedy Ann. So much to figure out! – Juan would rephrase a wise Chilean saying which was often written out on Chilean public buses over the long front mirror above the driver, "*Padres hay muchos, madre hay una sola*": "There are plenty of bottoms and only a few tops, darling – and that goes for men and women."

But I had found a connection with Andrew, a true raconteur. He was fidgety, bright, beautiful, and, for an Anglo, oddly curious about the world beyond his nose. I called him "a born again *Latino*." He had traveled through Central America and lived all over Colombia and Costa Rica, where he had effortlessly acquired his impeccable Spanish. When I came back from New York and into this lively household, I realized how much I enjoyed his company. Though I had met him and Garth briefly before my departure to Cuba, I realized that I had dedicated a number of letters to Andrew while I was away, and with his sweet replies he had crept into my heart. Once the sexual tension was over, we began to spend a lot of time together, over long breakfasts, telling stories, mixing words with strange spells; his wiry presence was warm and stimulating. I think Andrew was the one who first made me think I could actually be a student in Vancouver, I could be intelligent in a different language; before then, the idea seemed impossible. For Andrew, bright as he was, having late nights, working overtime, smoking lots of weed, and still getting by brilliantly with exams and papers, seemed effortless. I looked up to him, tall, beautiful, and carefree – and I confided in him. I told Andrew everything, including what I had just learned a few days earlier.

The doctor had told me I was HIV positive. My first thought was living, to live life, to live to the fullest, *vivir la vida*, the delicious promiscuity, a thought that was rapidly eclipsed by a nimbus of Catholic guilt, *no, hay que vivir el purgatorio*, the atonement of the sins of the flesh. I more or less forced myself to think I deserved it. *¡Mea culpa, por mi gran culpa, por la gran puta culpa!* When I cried, I did it more out of a sense of duty or protocol than out of shame or desperation. I dug deep for tempered feelings, but they weren't really in me at all. So wrapped up was I in these thoughts that I ignored the doctor's comment, something along the lines of "one more immigrant who comes here to die," and I concentrated on what I saw as his better qualities. However, the brutality of his "post-test counseling" was to echo loudly on my mind for many days to come. Later that day, still in a daze, I called Juan and broke the news to him.

"*Soy HIV positivo*," I blurted out dryly. Silence at the other end, and then. . . .

"Well . . . who isn't? Live it up, *lola. ¡Por donde pecas, pagas!*" Okay, I thought, I can live with that wisdom. When I phoned Cesar, I found that Italo was staying at his place while Cesar was away in Miami. Italo could not snap out of his pretentious and prissy Chilean queen self to utter even half a platitude. I sighed. Cesar and I had known Italo for fucking ever, he was always the same, he was family after all – all my sisters and me – a relative everybody tolerates because blood is thicker than water. Today Italo had only dirt to say about some *Marielito ordinario* who had crossed him. He had fucked him about a week before – much against his instincts, I thought – because he was a second-rate manager from the Met and had promised to get him tickets for the current season. Italo simply adored opera, he lived for it, he would kill or spread his legs for it. I was vulnerable that day, I waited to get a word in edgewise and I told him my news. It didn't spark much interest. After a few muttered words, he went on about how marrying a guy worth some money should now be my priority. I blurted out a quick goodbye and hung up.

I caught up with Cesar in Miami. He was staying with – of all people – Mariana Nomeolvides, hardly *la santa favorita de su devoción,* but
necessity knows no pride – *la necesidad tiene cara de hereje.* And Cesar
had to ask Mariana to put him up for a few days. Cesar had met
Mariana one of the few times that he had set foot in *El Goce Pagano*
– The Profane Satisfaction – Mariana's gay nightclub in Santiago, a
cheesy joint that operated in semi-clandestine fashion on weekends,
a place Cesar considered distasteful – *poco decente* – to say the least. She
had kicked him out for openly criticizing the locale, her attire, and
her boyfriend. Now, she was living in Miami with a new dubious
boyfriend, a cartoonish man with greased jet black hair, a gold cap on
one of his front teeth, some sort of Cuban Steven Seagal with a pronounced swagger, coke-induced staying power, and a long record for
drug trafficking. Cesar had flown down to Miami on short notice to
get his papers as a legal alien from some crooked lawyer and could
not think of anyone else to stay with. A cheap motel wasn't an option
for Cesar's heightened sense of style. He sounded indignant when I
told him the news.

"Go out and neuter the asshole who infected you!"

"It wasn't an *asshole* but a *cock* that infected me. I don't even know
who the father is! *Me pasó por puta.*" Cesar didn't think this was funny.
We talked for a while, and before he hung up he said that he would
"deal with me" as soon as he got back to New York, one of his moth-
ering statements that sounded worse than the diagnosis.

I couldn't blame Cesar for his outburst, he was under a lot of stress.
That trip to Miami was make-it-or-break-it for him. He paid a small
fortune, all his bank savings, to get a lawyer to process his application
papers, but when he went to the dreaded appointment the immigration officer told him point blank that he was lying. Unbeknownst to
him, the felonious lawyer had submitted an application under a special amnesty program for illegal fruit pickers in Florida. Cesar surely

didn't look anything like a Salvadoran or Mexican peasant! He broke down and begged on his knees – not an unusual genuflection for any practicing Catholic – telling the officer how he had religiously paid all those years of taxes, and that he had an impeccable, albeit illegally obtained, line of credit, every credit card there was, and not a single overdue payment – *muy decente*. He also swore on the grave of his dead mother – alive and well in Santiago – that he had never been in trouble with the law, and added, for good measure, that there was a pregnant American girlfriend in Manhattan waiting for him to come back home. The immigration officer, who could have had him deported right there and then, seemed impressed by the sheer diligence of this young man and told him that he would let him stay just because he looked honest. I don't think he believed the pregnant girlfriend bit, though. Later, Cesar would reflect that this had been his rite of passage into immigrant maturity and a quick goodbye to many Chilean compulsions. He had dressed down, lied through his Catholic teeth, and given a sour blow job to a stranger to get what he needed. Worst of all, he had followed what he considered Italo's most immoral advice: "*Un culo bien administrado rinde mucho mas que una mina de oro*" – one often sits on a million bucks, honey, don't waste it!

A week later, Juan called to tell me he too was going to Miami for an immigration interview to get his illegal alien status. He had heard about what had happened with Cesar so he smartened up and didn't take a shower, clip his nails, or shave for days. He was fully prepared to go the extra mile and carried a small bottle of Listerine in the pocket of the most worn-out jacket he could find. However, Juan wasn't as fortunate as Cesar. His female immigration officer interrogated him for an hour. Finally, she ordered him to be tested for HIV and to come back with the results. Juan knew what the results of this test would be, so he had to beg Mariana's staunch homophobe lover to walk into a free clinic and get tested under Juan's name. But when

Juan went back with the negative test results in hand, things didn't get any better. This officer simply wasn't buying it. When the interview took an ugly turn Juan asked to go to the bathroom, vomited, and by hoisting himself out a small window, left the building, the area, and his dreams of becoming legit in Miami that very evening.

Not unlike what my friends had done in Miami, it took me some manoeuvering to weasel my way into the sanctity of a Canadian university. I didn't want to be left behind. My housemates seem to be having so much fun as students, out and going places, shopping for stuff with their student loans. I decided to try it, although I wasn't very interested in burning my precious eyelashes reading books, the thought of meeting an intellectual and athletic Romeo was enticing. However, it took a good dose of elbow grease to get past the scrutiny of the university admissions officer. In those days there was nothing like a broken *Latino* English accent to soften the stiffness of petty bureaucrats. There weren't too many *Latinos* in Vancouver, so our profile was still exotic. I guess, in a way, I might have helped cement our reputation. Not knowing where to turn – Sol was too legit for any of these moves – I called Miami, our *Latino* centre of scam intelligentsia, to get tips from Mariana Nomeolvides on how to translate my Chilean academic transcripts and "enhance" them so I wouldn't have to start from zero again.

I also landed a job at a Jewish catering place on 4th Avenue owned by Susan, who didn't change her designer's blue linen ensemble for months at a time, and Deborah, a princess who spent more time on a plane than on firm ground. I served stale, overpriced *hors d'oeuvres* at uppity parties for a long while, always invoking my disco mantra *I've got so much love to give / I've got so much life to live / I will survive / I will survive, hey-hey!* I wasn't going to mope around or go on Prozac. I wasn't going to throw in the towel before the fat lady had truly sung, oh no, not me.

"May I freshen your drink, ma'am?" (What a lush!) I had learned the servant ropes from my mother in Chile and had also learned that each morning, no matter what, no matter who, one has to get up, put oneself together, and keep on going.

"These are tempura baby organic squash, sir." (As if you needed more cholesterol, you fat pig.)

Sitting at home and waiting patiently for the grim reaper to fetch me wasn't a choice, although I really didn't have a home, a niche, a place to seek shelter from the oppressive parochial liberalism of this town. Politicians and businessmen were trumpeting Vancouver as "a world class city" for the upcoming Expo '86, but under that *nouveau riche* veneer there was still a tight-assed town and queers were similarly proper and guarded.

"My apologies, sir, I didn't hear you, I will bring you a serviette right away." (I wish I could lick the dip from your pants myself, you arrogant, hot prick). However, sex with men was a dangerous proposition in Vancouver. This virus thing had queers even more scared – frankly, who needs a nervous queer? We are an insecure pretension of flamingos to begin with. The type of men I craved would be too straight to allow themselves some fun; corn-fed and schooled in hockey violence, they seem more prone to release their energies gaybashing than by letting a queer milk their testosterone. Ahh, Chile under a dictatorship, lots of stiff uniforms idly guarding the city, those were the days!

"I will personally refill the lox platter, ma'am. I assure you our utensils are ab-so-lu-tely hygienic." (I wish you'd back the fuck off, you tacky *hija de puta*, you ain't that classy anyway. As if I haven't already seen you pop three pills in two hours.) "My pleasure, ma'am."

And, there was the weirdest silence among queers. Vancouverites have always confused politeness with secrecy and if one had the audacity of being upfront about HIV, it made gay men leave skid marks on the pavement. The whole city was a big AIDS closet and HIV had put a tight lock on it.

"Care for an infection, sir — I mean, a confection?" (*Ojos que no ven, corazón que no siente* dear, if you had only seen the kitchen where they were cooked.) I was already enrolled in school and attending classes, but studying and sashaying around with heavy trays in the evenings was not a living. Something had to happen.

A few months after my return to Vancouver, I met Roger. I answered his personal ad in *Angles*, the local gay newspaper. It was all weird and fast, we met, he looked familiar, he was a professor at the university, I had seen him before, but I didn't think he was gay. He inspected me intensely — I thought it was "intensity," but it was a wandering eye — and then we fucked the entire afternoon, messy and heavy. I stayed the night and skipped classes the day after. I was tied up as it were. I called in sick at the catering place the following evening, left more imprints of my back against a table, a counter, an area rug, the mud in the back yard at night. I left the house three days later, worn out. A month after my HIV diagnosis I went back to the same doctor — why fight him, I thought, what was the point of fighting docs anyway? They have us by the balls most of the time. This doctor and I needed to make some history, get used to each other. He inquired about a couple of small bluish bruises on my buttocks. I blushed, muttered hurried explanations, he wouldn't let go, and sent me for further tests immediately. Why make such a fuss about a few well-placed welts on my ass, I thought. A week later, I moved in with Roger leaving behind an astonished Sol and a doubtful Andrew. Another week passed. I kissed the catering business goodbye and went to see the doctor once more only to hear that my spleen was enlarged, HIV-related, no sound explanation. I had to have a splenectomy. I told the doctor I had met Roger and was living with him, to which he huffed that he knew exactly who I was talking about. I thought he was jealous — *el perro del hortelano, no come, ni deja comer.*

Numbed, I went back to Roger's that day, my new domicile, and broke the news to him. In lieu of consolation, he fucked me and when we were getting cleaned up he told me he had to travel abroad for business for two months. In passing, he told me his previous lover had died in that house only a month before he had met me. Such news! That explained the dark sculptures and ink drawings around the house and the stack of grisly Polaroids in the library. I realized that Roger and I had never had much of a conversation about anything before I moved into his old house in Strathcona. I only had a week before the hospital to worry about being a substitute for the one who was now pushing up daisies. They cut me up; a big slash too! Roger came to see me come to my senses after the operation. Garth, Andrew, and Sol were there too and their chemistry with Roger was a bit tense, or so I surmised from behind my veil of morphine. Three days later, a nurse came in and pulled the tubes from my nose with a single yank. I fainted. I woke up feeling woozy and surrounded by bouquets of flower like a virgin in a shrine. Roger was gone on his conference trip. I honeymooned alone and high on painkillers. *¡Ave Maria purisima, sin pecado concebida!*

My close friends behaved like jealous lovers. They took turns giving me sermons about moving in with Roger so quickly.

"You might lose in this deal," Andrew said.

"Lose what? Sleep? I have nothing. It's like that Shirley Bassey song: 'I who have nothing/I who have no one/I adore you –'"

"I get it, I get it – but Roger seems so . . . intense."

"I find that sexually attractive, yes, and the fact that he is some twenty years my senior. He's wise, he's got connections. He's already talking about me going to graduate school. He teaches there, you know."

"*Lo que Roger tiene es dinero.*" Andrew could nail it on the head in both my official languages.

"I beg your pardon! I'm in *love . . . and* he has money, I'll give you *that.*"

Roger's house was a narrow wooden structure in Strathcona near Chinatown that had been built in the early 1900s by Chinese immigrants. It was cluttered with paintings, appliances, and books. It also housed an interminable saga of memories; the Chinese ghosts of entire generations covered everything like layers of dried skin. I could feel their presence. I could hear the *mahjong* tiles clacking against each other. In a note to my friend Chela in Santiago I wrote: *En esta casa de Strathcona rondan los fantasmas, los de los chinos son desgreñados, ruidosos y juguetones; el del difunto es pesado y lento, no se quiere ir, son sus celos quizá, está suspendido en el aire enrarecido, el muy hijo de puta, detenida está su alma en las fotos y las cartas. Un dia cuando estaba husmeando en los estantes de la oficina volqué la urna con las cenizas del difunto. Las reuní con un cepillo y muchas oraciones y la puse de vuelta. Tuve miedo de las represálias de ultratumba por haberme mudado a esa casa con demasiado apuro.* Chela responded in her dreadful English handwriting and usual blasé manner that superstition was the opiate of the masses – a catch-all Marxist phrase he had learned from his young lover Uli. Chela claimed the most important thing was that I had a man with big guns, tools, and a chequing account.

ROGER WAS GONE FOR A COUPLE OF LONG WINTER months. In those days of convalescence Andrew and Camilo, sensually resting on a *tableau vivant* over the bed, began to tell stories to each other — their hands drawing chinoiserie in the air — to keep the ghosts of the Strathcona Street house at bay. Andrew told how long and painful it had been for him to get Garth to love him; how he had been saving himself for Garth since high school. He had patiently appeased Garth's prairie reluctance and showed him a road out of the northern town of Dawson Creek where Garth insisted he was content. Andrew thought his world was complete when Garth came to Vancouver to join him. But Andrew told Camilo about how Garth, the son of rich prairie ranchers, had always intimately made him feel self-conscious about being "white trash," the fourth son of an alcoholic mother and a father who had abandoned them when they were all young. Camilo said that he would take a trailer queen as a friend over a prissy, high-brow queen anytime, and told him how out of place he always felt growing up, feelings he had been shedding like old layers of skin over the years in Canada, replacing them with new feelings of immigrant inadequacy. Camilo was an only child, the sissy out-of-wedlock son of a live-in maid, always by himself, daydreaming, reading, and writing in the maid's quarters, stashed away in a corner of the large and elegant houses where his mother worked incredibly long days. Those were houses full of stylish objects, inhabited by lovely, tasteful, sophisticated adults and troubled ghosts.

"How is that situation any different from being in this house?" Andrew asked at one point, and when he saw Camilo get flustered he realized the poignancy of his question. They moved on. Another evening while it poured outside, Andrew recounted his long and tedious redneck Alberta childhood, the liberal touchy-feely 1960s, the day his father abandoned them to try his luck in New Zealand.

Andrew thought he would die because he felt deeply connected to that bearded, pensive man. More so than his sisters, Andrew had found an oasis from the constant drudgery of their lives in the few moments they shared together, when they did boy things in which his sisters were not included. He cherished and protected those moments from others because he had learned how comforting that loving could be, how mysterious, and how envy could turn it into something dirty. When his father had departed without even saying goodbye, Andrew felt something had been arrested, something had been stolen, and what was left inside of him he kept secret until he met Garth in high school. Andrew described the rest of his childhood as days of winter frost and summer suffocation, always gathering up their few belongings in worn-out suitcases and hauling them to the next town, always depending on the disdainful charity of others. It seemed that they were perpetually riding in their old red Rambler with his mother and his sisters, always moving, always on welfare, under an interminable sky with no horizon in sight, before finally hitting one more town.

"Are you ever afraid Garth might do this to you?" The sudden glimpse of anxiety in Andrew's eyes made Camilo aware of his unfortunate choice of words. They changed the subject and poured another mug of orange pekoe.

Camilo recounted stories of the riots, *las protestas de las ollas vacias*, he remembered the resolute women marshalling the columns of people, banging pots and pans down the street protesting the shortage of food brought about by American meddling in Chilean internal affairs; getting hosed down by water cannons, suffocated by tear gas bombs. He was a child running among the young protesters, unafraid, having fun until sunset, knowing he would be scorned by his mother for staying out all day. His curiosity was piqued by the burly men with thick beards, who held their women by their narrow waists, protective, yelling angrily, fists raised in the air. On demonstration days, Camilo

traveled up and down the occupied streets mesmerized by the forest
of straining arms and legs, the columns of necks. He remembered getting close enough to get a whiff of their intense sweat, circling those
agitated men at a careful distance when they sat exhausted on the
curb, having dropped their torn banners and thrown the remaining
stacks of pamphlets in the air like doves.

Camilo described the lack of food and the long lines, *las colas*, to get
the daily bread or a ration of meat or sugar or oil. He could visualize
the day of the *coup d'état* on September 11, 1973, and how the rich
people his mother worked for celebrated in the streets the very same
morning that many of those agitators had begun to be exterminated.
Using a Hitlerian military falsetto in his many speeches, a perennial-
ly irate General Pinochet called those communist and socialist men
and women *sediciosos* and *subversivos*, the maggots within the tradi-
tionally decent and devout Chilean society. Camilo remembered the
incessant barking of machine gun fire in the nights, the muffled stomp
of soldiers like runaway horses on the sidewalks, the planes descend-
ing low into the city, instilling terror in poor people in *poblaciones*
where many of his mother's friends lived. Many of these friends,
grassroots or union activists, were imprisoned, fired from their jobs,
or silenced in other ways. Uptown, while lining up for a few scarce
provisions, Camilo's mother would receive only quick reports delivered in hushed tones from other maids in the neighbourhood. In the
tough years that followed the coup, Camilo and his mother moved
often through various households. In this world of uniformed and
hardened grimaces, silence and discipline were salvation. Being a *maricón* didn't really matter much, certainly not to the many *soldados*
armed to the teeth and clad in green camouflage gear and leather. The
armed forces had bigger and better enemies. As Camilo grew up and
took longer detours home from school, or stayed out in the streets
later into the evening after he was finished school, he learned that

many soldiers were uprooted for long periods of time, were far away from their rural hometowns, and they were lonely – and horny.

"You learned a few things over those years," Andrew reflected after a long pause.

Camilo exhaled a deep sigh. "Yeah, that the way you are brought up is the way you fuck."

IN THOSE LONG CONVERSATIONS NESTLED UNDER the blankets to temper the cold evenings and through the sudden chills and fever of my convalescence, I told Andrew why I had done the things I had thus far done in my life: mostly out of insolence, resentment, and envy, I think. More out of chance than design. Many of the things I did flew in the face of Chilean convention. In a country shepherded by an omniscient and omnipotent Catholic God who had a tight grip on our genitals and our souls, a country in which social class seems genetically inscribed and more significant than the wealth one could ever amass, my knee-jerk reactions must have looked like a flamboyant tourette. The upper classes hate *nouveau riche* more than they hate the working class. The lower classes represent no menace. The greedy and fickle Chilean middle class, filled with pretensions, would do anything to get what my mother called "a whiff of decency" and, more importantly, to whiten their past against the mix with *Mapuche* blood. Who was to know that many years later a similar *nouveau riche* attitude could still almost make me gag while serving canapés among Vancouver's finest *nouveau riche* from Hong Kong and upper Indian castes trying so hard to couch their skin in garish furniture and sparkling sedans?

But my *mestizo* class would always betray me as I grew up, I couldn't hide the telltale shade of my skin. The same shading would prove to be an asset in the future or, at times, an impediment. Who was to know that many years later I would live in a place in which a similar scorn for shade would make people support what they called multiculturalism? However, it wasn't the shade of my skin that worried me then in Chile, but its cha-cha rhythm. As time went by, my body could hardly harness my frenetic spirit, it would erupt all through my bones and skin and its movements, loud and flashy, in a whirlwind, batting my eyelashes at men, laughing loudly, dressing in ways that were considered unbecoming for a man. In other words, I had slowly bloomed into being *el maricón del barrio.* What family or neighbourhood doesn't have its own swishy black sheep? How can normal be without *una oveja descarriada?* Of course, I wasn't the only one; like me, there were many bold flaming queens defying convention and good masculine manners, but I was intensely ambitious, insolent, sharp, and restless. *¡A mi no me callaba nadie!* I wanted to know and see more and I acquired what I wanted in a social black market of memories. I didn't dutifully keep my place on the social ladder. I aimed for married, middle-class Catholic men, professionals, soldiers, men who would feel entitled to sow really wild oats once in a blue moon – *un desliz lo tiene cualquiera* – I can even count a cabinet minister under my belt. "Straight" men, in fact, many men make interesting lovers although they have strange rules: kissing is out of bounds, it's too intimate (but they will stick their tongue up anyone's ass); fucking young men is not really being a homosexual, it's simply getting one's rocks off. I used to think that swallowing their seed was almost like taking communion and that only the most missionary of penetrations amounted to real sex. This all happened – I should clarify – way before spit and raw skin went out of style. As soon as my fleeting lovers had released their seed, they fled the scene. I can't count all the times in which I was unceremoniously kicked out of moving cars in desolate places, left on the curb, clenching a couple of bills like the ruffled feathers of a hen. Other times I wasn't so lucky, and later, explaining bruises or black eyes to my mother was very difficult. It was always the middle class guys who would freak out the worst. The working class guys, the soldiers, the low ranking police officers, proved to be tough but reliable lovers who would come around a second and third time. Some even offered to set me up as a *querida,* apartment and all. I wanted the comfort, and the alimony, but I appreciated my freedom too much. During those years, I took what I needed to put myself through university and become a teacher – don't get me wrong, I also worked odd jobs, polished and waxed floors in fancy houses, worked as a courier on foot downtown, and when I learned enough English I was hired as a tour guide during the summers to shepherd unsuspecting tourists around and tell them a pack of lies. I was a jack-of-all-trades-and-tricks, as it were.

IN ROGER'S HOUSE ON PENDER STREET, ANDREW and the convalescent Camilo mapped for each other the roads that had led them to Vancouver. Probably the only thing that separated them in those days was Camilo's need to rest after a long day and the fresh line that traced the surgeon's scalpel. Otherwise, both friends were like children, entranced by the telling of the stories. Camilo told Andrew how running against the current was in his nature. His mother had done it when she was very young. In a world in which she had almost nothing, barely a pair of shoes, she had painstakingly saved money for the train ticket to escape being a shepherd in *Nueva Imperial*, the south of Chile, to travel to the capital. She was the youngest of ten children of an impoverished family, and according to tradition, she was to take care of her mother until the end of her days. Instead, she had left. She was twenty then. After a few years of being in the service of an uptown family in Santiago, Camilo's mother had done the unspeakable: she had allowed the young *patrón* of the house, a two-bit Don Juan, to consummate his daily advances. She soon regretted her wavering will when she realized that her period was late, but not being one prone to sentimentalism, she recovered promptly and made the difficult decision not to get a back alley abortion, so common in those days, and to keep her child. She told her *patrona* that she had met a policeman, a young *Mapuche* from *Temuco* now serving in Santiago, a common occurrence even today, and that he was the father of the child-to-be, that he said that he would marry her later. The *patrona* did not bat an eyelash, accustomed as she was that maids would always come out with a "surprise," what was inexplicably termed "*un domingo siete*;" she gave Camilo's mother-to-be a stern look, told her not to miss too much work, to deal with it when the time came, and never to give her another "disappointment" such as this. However, not quite a year after Camilo was born, he began to show some resemblance to the young *patrón* and by the time Camilo was four, not even the most resolute Chilean blind eye could overlook some apparent facts. Camilo had clearly inherited the stubborn coyness of his *Mapuche* mother – a soft wind wrapped around a menacing tempest – and from her he had received the smooth caramel of his *moreno* skin, the prominent cheek-bones, the small square hands and the thick blackness of the hair and the eyelashes. Nevertheless, the deep green hue of his irises and their intense glare betrayed the presence of a father of Germanic descent. In view of such a resemblance, one day, Camilo's mother was quietly told to leave.

I GUESS THE FRUIT DOESN'T FALL FAR FROM THE TREE. I wasn't a "good liberated homosexual." I didn't much care for others like me, my *loca* friends were good for the *carrete*, but not for romance. I craved married men, even with all their baggage; they were more reliable and resourceful in their intimacy. I wasn't the good son of a maid who becomes a loyal house gardener and pool boy. I wanted to go and study, not in a vocational school as everyone kept on repeating to me, where working class boys should go, but I insisted on going to a *liceo* and then to a university. And after I graduated, I wasn't a good dutiful teacher; my school colleagues disapproved of me because I wasn't political enough, I was more concerned with colour co-ordination than with Marxist critical dialectics, and I was too effeminate. But my students, the boys and girls in my first high school job in *Pudahuel*, told me they didn't care about who was going to bed with whom at all as long as one kept it to oneself, but on more than one occasion, girls and boys alike offered me consolation which I gently turned down — well, not always.

I loved teaching but the poverty and mediocrity of public schools horrified me. Even with my two paltry full-time salaries, I couldn't put together enough money to rent a decent place and move away from my modest abode in *Calle Carmen* where I lived since I had turned fifteen. That was when the *patrona* of the house my mom and I lived in walked in on me and her precious *kosher* seventeen-year-old son perched on my back, humping like a deranged dog. Needless to say, she was absolutely *fartulmt*. It may have been because it was the week between Rosh Hashanah and Yom Kippur, but I think she was more horrified about the dangling *escapulario* on my *goyish* neck than about our grotesque entanglement, and her damned cocker spaniel!

In any case, everything was dealt with in the traditional Chilean low-key demeanor – fortunately, my mom didn't lose her job, room, and board, but I had to go.

I don't recall sleeping very often during my university years – *¡Hice de la noche, dia, y de la vida una fiesta!* – Santiago's gay nightlife was seedy and hidden, but it vibrated like a rattlesnake. At that time, the circulating stories about disco clubs in New York, the blond well-hung *gringos*, the blow jobs, and the good jobs were legendary. The boys in my street clique would recount them and enhance them, while putting together coins to go clubbing Thursday, Friday, and Saturday nights. *Todas ibamos a ser reinas / lo decíamos embriagadas / y lo tuvimos por verdad.* We had all read the poems, we had memorized all the lyrics, we had seen all the movies! One of us left first. I guess it was Italo; he was the most entrepreneurial and had carefully managed his ass to get a ticket and a hard-to-come-by tourist visa. After a few years, it was my turn and, again, I went against the social script of the good *mariquita* child and left my single mother behind to go abroad to try my luck. Still ringing in my ears are the many voices telling me that I couldn't go at all, that I had to take care of my mother in her old age just as she had taken care of all my needs as I grew up. My mother was the only one who never joined that fastidious choir.

"You can only survive in spite of others, *lola,*" were some of Juan's famous last words. *¿Cómo olvidarlo?* I guess that is the essence of writing one's life against the script. Cesar, Juan, and even Italo, who had been coaxed into contributing some cash, felt betrayed by me too. Cesar, in particular, who had gone to New York two years earlier, worked hard and saved every penny to pay my ticket from Santiago to Narita, Japan, a flight that had a stopover in Vancouver where I would get off – such was our plan – walk out of the airport, and find a contact who would drive me across the border to Seattle, supposedly an easy passage by car at that time. In Seattle, I would catch a Greyhound to New York. This never happened. The very night I arrived in Vancouver I was told there was a way to stay, no one said it was fully legitimate, but it made me have a change of heart. It was Mariana who planted the seed. What she was doing in this neck of the woods, I never knew. I have never asked. She didn't even live in Vancouver, she was just passing through. In any case, her highly wrought web of stories made me see that I didn't want to live illegally for years in a foreign country. I wasn't fully aware of what that was like. I could only imagine it, but, again, I rode on loads of happy-go-lucky intuition. I stayed in Vancouver, sometimes regretting it later, but for the most part, I learned to live with the consequences. My staying in Vancouver deeply disappointed Cesar in New York, but he did not hold a grudge for long and we never lost contact. It was only years later that I had the chance to sit face to face with each one of them in New York and make amends.

In those days of convalescence, the phone rang insistently – Cesar, Juan, Sol, Andrew, Garth, and Roger phoned all the time. Chela also phoned often from Santiago, collect of course, and we chatted animatedly for hours, dishing about Mariana, Cesar, and Italo. She said that she was concerned about my health but she also assured me that I was strong, *la mala hierba nunca muere*, and she was glad to hear about my new *marido*, his house, and other impressive attributes. Chela and I had met through a mutual friend barely forty-eight hours after her arrival in Santiago on New Year's eve 1980. I instantly spotted a girlfriend in her. I quickly got past her tacky polyester outfits and the size of her hands. Not once did I feel attracted to her, a good sign – believe you me, there were not many living creatures I didn't feel attracted to at that age! She was oddly interested in talking about politics, which was *not* a concern among the young wannabe queens in

Chile. So little did they care about politics that *I* was pinned as the radical element in our pack. Imagine that! Ahh, queers, so often the ambivalent escorts of fascism.

Chela, *la gringa*, has never made it to Vancouver. She comes up with one excuse after the other – doesn't have the money to fly, doesn't find the time, Uli might be cheating on her, blah, blah. She'd never admit it that she'd rather not see me. I am, after all, one of the few remaining human beings who could truly remember her story. If I croak, her story dies with me. Chela, was . . . different at that time, a *gringo* from Washington, DC, who went to Chile for two weeks in 1980 on a dare; a couple of weeks stretched into years. Her truth, being stranger than fiction, was that she fell in love with Uli, a young lad who made a buck on weekend nights by guarding cars parked outside *El Goce Pagano*. On one of those nights, he momentarily stepped in from the cold to get a hot cup of tea from the bartenders who took pity on him and he happened to see Chela in a sequined dress, drunk and disheveled, lanky, pale, glamorous in her own decadent, late Farrah Fawcett way. It was show time! Uli was enraptured. Chela was beside herself and gave up his cherished schedules, the Protestant work ethic – *that* was easy – and both of his balls to stay in Santiago and live the life of queens. "*Chela, la gringa, triunfadora y divina. ¿Cómo no envidiarla? En cambio a mi se me ocurrió vivir mi vida como la Virginia Slims, agringada, independiente y decidida.* "I had to come to see what the American Dream was all about, encouraged by Chela. I promised myself to go back in four years tops, not rich, but smiling, but got caught up in a maze of small detours. Chela and I were migrants to opposite latitudes, two extremities of the same desire to invent ourselves, one in the face of American absurdity and the other in the face of historical adversity.

"We were all to be queens," wrote *la Mistral*, *"de cuatro reinos sobre el mar"* and, yes, our dream came true, but in odd ways. Chela and I began to pull all-nighters in my stark adobe room in *Calle Carmen.* We talked about everything, in broken tongues, taking turns to learn salacious idioms from each other, "dishing" about our fleeting lovers as we sipped tea from a steaming pot perched on the small kerosene heater that doubled as a stove. Every evening starting at around nine: we would hold court for a small entourage of young queens who would come around much to the chagrin of my emphysemic, chain-smoking landlady, a wrinkled old hag and former prostitute, who would once in a while snap and chase us all into the street yelling, *"Maricones, desviados, pervertidos, poco hombres,"* maddened by our high-school girl giggles. Sometimes she would ambush me in the early morning when I was trying to tiptoe back to my stingy room with a prince I had found ambling under the early morning stars and demand the always late rent payment, and predict that my Romeo *du jour* and I would burn in the eternal fires of hell. Indeed, we warmed up those frosty morning hours considerably. Indeed, we all ended up in hell.

On one of those interminable nights, Chela confided to me that she had made the radical decision to go through "the change" to be with Uli forever. She said that Uli wanted this. I gasped, "Chop it? Forever? *Gringa,* you are fucking insane!" I protested. For weeks on end, I warned Chela that men are lovely but not reliable. I argued, "We are Catholics, we are carefree – not to mention Uli is so young. Say, I fall in love every hour on the hour. Sure, it is for real, but it ain't lasting." Chela wouldn't listen, she only praised me on my impeccable use of the slang "ain't." I warned him, er . . . her, that *Chilenos* are good before they get married, when they have to make an effort at romance. Then they get bored or distracted and find themselves a mistress, man, woman, whoever. Why would she split from her *huevos*? They are, after all, what keep you afloat in this world that is so fucking nasty to girls. Finally, I told her to be practical, to think of how hard it would be to make a decent living in Chile. I reminded her how she hardly made it to the end of the month by teaching English to pretentious uptown jackasses in a cheesy language academy. I reminded her of the malls, household appliances, credit cards, cars, hot running water, all the things she had in Washington DC that we didn't have in Santiago. Of course, this argument backfired because these were the things I didn't have and I wanted for myself, not what Chela wanted in her future. I needed my *cojones* to get them! She didn't. "But, I have to be me! I've always wanted to be me," was her response. I sighed and told her that I would support her forever. Inside I thought, Fuck this shit! Chela wants Uli because he is a starving Communist offspring. In a weird way the kid is some sort of political trophy for a political *gringa*. Then I thought I was going nuts, talking to myself like that. What *gringa*? There was no *gringa*! But, that story will remain in the past forever, together with Chela's *huevos*.

It would be years before I met Uli; I sized him up, and saw what bang he gave Chela for her buck, a long-term investment, that's for sure. At the time I was making friends with Chela, Uli refused to be around us, calling us *locas perdidas* or *maricones patéticos*. Later, he warmed up. Uli, short for Lenin's last name Vladimir Ilich Ulianov – an implausible name even in a country where the working class is populated by Matthew Tapias, Ronald Zepedas, and Marilyn Catrileos – had been registered as such by an eager communist single mother who never went through the petit bourgeois process of baptizing him. She had been *disappeared* in the late '70s along with other political prisoners. Uli's grandmother had raised him with a progeny of foster daughters and sons. The disillusioned grandmother had become a devout Jehovah's Witness and preached to the children day and night. Thus, Uli would periodically freak out and fall out of sight, which made Chela's mascara bleed in despair. She said that her entrepreneurial colonizing *gringo* spirit had made her persevere. Chela always explained carefully how she had closed her squalid U.S. chequing accounts, she had emotionally blackmailed her Anglican parents to get some more dough, one last call before the day of the final judgment, put together penny by penny, found a cheap doctor in Miami who would bypass what Chela diagnosed as "silly and redundant psychiatric interviews for gender reassignment" and got admitted there several times over a year. Much to my dismay, she insisted on taking on a tacky name like "Chela" because she said it better identified her with *her* people who would have a hard time writing "Sheila." However, she never polished her accent in Spanish or darkened her frizzy, bleached blonde hair. Back in Santiago, one day after she had a round of hormone injections at a local private clinic, I told Chela I had just received a letter from Andrew telling me there was a way, and money, to join him in New York.

"Pack up and go," Chela said. "I know, I know – your mother, your vocation, your calling, your career, face it, teaching in Chile is for the birds. Darling, look at you, you work and work and work and live in this dive. It'll be years before you get one single decent job. You'll be a cranky old queen by then. There is an American girl screaming to get out of you. Darling, all these years of watching poorly dubbed reruns of *Charlie's Angels* will not have been spent in vain! Go."

CAMILO HAD STORED HUNDREDS OF CHELA'S LETTERS. Their prolific correspondence throughout the years became a journal in which they sketched, line by line, their immigrant saga, Camilo's diagnosis, fears, and torrid affairs, Chela's metamorphosis, and the ebbs and flows of her romance with Uli from *La Serena*. The kid, as Camilo had accurately predicted, kept her heart like a bird on a wire, leaping from one mood to another. His family and his girlfriend back home didn't know he was gay. In his mind, he was just humouring a drag queen. He wouldn't let her touch him, he would tease her, get her to dine him and wine him, to pay for his basic needs; it didn't trouble him at all, but it surely troubled Chela. Uli refused to stay in Santiago permanently and more so to live with Chela as she was pleading. Coyly, he said he couldn't leave his *abuela Rubelinda*; it would break her heart. Therefore, Chela was caught in her first woman-to-woman struggle, a long distance one. She knew that Uli's *abuela* suspected something about his student life in Santiago, that the boarding house that belonged to a landlady with a heart of gold where Uli said he lived for next to nothing in Santiago was just a story – Chela knew that the *abuela* knew. By Uli's account *Rubelinda* was putting up a good struggle to keep her grandson from making any final decision to leave *La Serena*. The *abuela* encouraged Uli's girlfriend to have a baby and get married, whatever would take place first – this in spite of the obvious contradiction to her strict evangelical precepts. Every time Uli stayed too long in Santiago or didn't call to report back to his family about his goings on, *abuela Rubelinda* would panic and her secular side would promptly take over her most pious practices. She would go around the house smudging and chanting to some Caribbean magical imports *Yemayá* and *Ochún* that she was told would be even more effective than the virgins of *La Tirana* and *La Candelaria*. At the peak of her desperation, the *abuela* summoned the

young girl that Uli was reluctantly dating when he was in *La Serena* and whispered a wise saying in her ear, a bit crass, but easily understood: *El hombre es fuego, la mujer es hierba, viene el diablo y sopla* – by far the most effective spell in the land. Uli's portentous member, a body part that functioned independently from his mind and heart, did get his girlfriend pregnant. On her side, Chela panicked and redoubled her female guile, presenting herself like a seductive Salome at every occasion she had, in spite of their shoddy surroundings. And although the deed was done, Chela did not give up and devised a new strategy. She convinced Uli to bring the girl to Santiago for a lovely early honeymoon. First, Uli brought pictures, and then, naïve as he was, he brought the girl to *Santiago*, over twelve hours by bus. Needless to say the girl, who had never been to Santiago, was utterly intimidated – and probably flabbergasted – at the sight of so many big buildings, cars, noises, and the big *gringa* friend of her consort (Uli's *abuela Rubelinda* had impressed upon the *La Serena* girl, that she was a consort). Chela was well warned that *un pelo del coño jala mas duro que una yunta de bueyes*, but she was one hundred percent woman too, and put up a shrewd struggle. Uli and the girl in *La Serena* did get married, but things had changed irreversibly after her visit to the capital; they never touched each other again, they never discussed the visit much, in fact, they never saw each other often.

As Chela blossomed in her femaleness, things began to look brighter for her. Initially she taught English to uptown teenagers in one of the many half-baked language institutes in Santiago staffed by displaced and dysfunctional *gringos* who were unable to make it in their own land and thus found shelter in the colonies. She was getting *really* tired of teaching when she reluctantly accepted moonlighting as a drag queen on weekends in the seedy but popular joint *El Goce Pagano*. Mariana Nomeolvides, who at that time was one of the owners of the place, saw in her a potential novelty act and cunningly persuaded her that this audience was "truly working class, the perfect public for your lofty ideas." Somehow, this turned into a full-time activity, which saved Chela from depression and incipient alcoholism. One day Mariana, acting as matchmaker, lured a begrudging Uli in to see the show. Uli's beautiful iron eyes widened as he saw such lewdness and mayhem. He was mortified when Chela blew him kisses from the stage in front of dozens of screeching creatures. After the show he resolutely marched backstage, trampling into the small dressing room packed with bellowing, half-naked queens with runs in their stockings and cheap *brisqué* that made them look like French pastries. He made a beeline to Chela and slapped her. It was a glorious slap that brought the usual dressing room pandemonium to a screeching halt. *¡Dios! ¡Tremendo chanchazo que le pegó a la gringa!* Next, Uli dragged her into the tiny bathroom and locked himself up with her. Many ears bedecked with *bijouterie* were pressed up against the old chipped door. The queens held their breath. Inside Uli lifted Chela's lovely gown and fucked her against the same chipped old door.

"*La suerte de la fea, la bonita la desea,*" whispered one of the other queens when she felt the vibrations.

"*No. La suerte de la gringa, la latina la desea,*" yelled Chela through the plywood, almost suffocated by Uli's eruption.

Later that year Uli stopped looking after parked cars outside *El Goce Pagano* and began to spend less time in *La Serena*. He also registered in high school to complete his education.

ULI WAS SO YOUNG, SO WAS I, BUT I WON'T TELL you how old Chela was. Young flesh is highly coveted, but *that* has never made me turn my head. Well-inhabited male bodies, like big, sturdy, and protective houses – that is what has always attracted me. Crow's feet around the eyes pull me towards men in the way that one is curious about opening old creaky windows into mysterious pasts. I love the coarse abrasions caused by salty skin and indomitable late evening stubble. I fancy my limbs bolstered around a man's architecture, *trenzados como mechas de india,* kneading, *enraizados en tierra firme,* yearning to be rooted. I love the basic awkwardness of tired muscles and beaten knuckles in which I can make tenderness happen. Like Chela, I was always driven to get the one I fancied. I mean, sometimes I wanted it so badly my body ached, a desire always unfilled since as long as I can remember. When I was a child I always talked to strangers; my mother says that the city and the strangers are comforting and safe. I liked learning things from strangers: gestures, ways of dressing to disguise or expose. But if our chemistry was wrong I got into pushing buttons. I could get away with that, often they would get fed up with my slew of impertinent questions and they would give me money to go away, or someone would invite me to eat something, or at least offer pity – it all depended on the yarn that I was spinning. I knew the game I played.

One incident in particular and what I learned from it stays on my mind. I might have been eleven or twelve – can't recall exactly – and it was a dark winter afternoon. I had stayed in the public library reading voraciously, as I often did. Then, on my way to the bus stop, I stumbled into a political rally in *Avenida Providencia* – one of those haphazardly organized, almost spontaneous demos against Pinochet that ended up in senseless screaming, clouds of tear gas, bloody faces, and nervous laughter, almost carnival-like. I knew my mom would be worried I had stayed out this late, but I also knew that she preferred to have me somewhere outside the overbearing atmosphere of the households she worked for. Somewhere where I could be protected from all that bullshit.

I know I looked cute in my *uniforme escolar*: grey pants, white starched shirt, blue jacket without lapels, and a school badge. I could easily pass for a little girl – I was an effeminate *moreno*, clean, soft-spoken, and nimble. I looked dutiful and innocent, polished in manners and attire, the product of the pristine discipline of the small charity *San Ramón* Catholic school, for boys only, mostly sons of *empleadas* and *obreros*. Oddly, the building was located in what had gradually become the fancy shopping area of *Providencia*. I guess I looked the oddest, standing there, mesmerized by the human traffic and its intensity, witnessing the yells, the stomping boots, and the sudden ebbs and flows of people, first attacking the *carabineros*, then retreating from the water cannons and the black and white armoured trucks. I felt no fear when I became part of the running herd and I ended up crouching behind a battered newsstand, clutching my brown leather school bag, holding close to a man. We stayed there for quite a while, panting, watching others scuttling back and forth in the midst of the chaos. I started to watch the man with flirtatious eyes – he was probably in his thirties, wet from head to toe, with dark stubble and dark eyelashes, and bad teeth protected by thick lips. I began to ask some silly questions in a low, meek voice, almost teasing, personal, with not as much as a tingling of butterflies in my stomach. Although he was impatient and he thought that I was an uptown boy – not a working class boy – he humoured me. I think that man was the first one to see the desire right through me, beginning to burn. An hour later, we had escaped the madness of *Avenida Providencia* and the danger of being clubbed by *carabineros* and dragged by the hair, and we drifted off to various side streets sheltered by the evening shadows. The truth is that I knew that neighbourhood like the palm of my hand – I used to spend a lot of time simply ambling the streets, daydreaming that I lived in those big, comfortable houses – and the man had come from a suburb to join the demonstration. I knew where I was taking him, he knew he was being led. There was little conversation, almost none. We reached an old residential building on a dark side street, and without any hesitation, I trespassed one of those front fences, I knew there was no guardian dog there, one of those vicious dogs that everyone used to have to protect the house at night. He followed me without a word. In the midst of an abundant front yard, protected by bushes and branches from the sight of possible passers-by and from the faint lights of the big house, the man's calloused hands crumpled my pristine shirt after he took it off. God, how feverish and long those fingers felt! With the same curiosity with which my classmates opened a new comic book, I undid his zipper. He tried to push me down on him, I was reluctant, and instead I kneaded his meat in amazement. He huffed, kept on looking around, alarmed, and quickly flipped me against a wide tree. Agitatedly, I undressed, brazen, not scared of being stark naked in the middle of a stranger's front garden. Then the man seized the fresh flower of my youth, which felt unlike anything I had felt before, like having a lizard crawl up my spine, viscous and hot. It was all going fine until I quickly turned around again, my pants and shorts half way down my legs, and I embraced him very tightly. The man flinched at the touch of my quivering lips but he responded timidly, then he put more of him into it. For a few fleeting moments, his heavy hand slightly caressed the nape of my neck. Again, I tried to kiss him and asked him if we could be lovers. I could feel his breath on my face – it stopped abruptly at the sound of the candid question. His eyes widened. He tried to push me away gently. I wouldn't let go. Visibly bowled over by my forwardness, he pushed me away and gave me a couple of rough shakes.

"What's with you? This is queer. *¡Chiquillo de mierda!* This is not normal. You fucking rich little faggot – trying to tempt me." His voice was not a careful whisper any longer; it could be audible from the house. I was in tears and trying to put myself together, my legs were shaking, my insides were red.

"But, you made love to me, just now."

"Fuck you, I never did such a thing, never," he snarled, while tucking his wet shirt into his pants. "I'm a man, forget it, this never happened, hear me?" He shook me again. "You little *maricones* should be disciplined, educated for the real life, not like fucking girls – real education, that's what this country needs." Then he turned around and left me in the thick of the wet yard. He didn't look back. I was no older than eleven or twelve. I would never forget.

I have always loved education, even though it is such as sado-masochistic affair – or maybe this is why I like it so much. It was only fortunate that I was sent to summer camp around the same time I was getting curious about men. *Solo Dios sabe* what could have happened to me! I had to learn a few lessons in seduction . . . and safety. The touch of men was forbidden in private, yet in public *machos* were allowed to be all over each other: in bars, in the soccer games when they had scored, in the hang-out corners of the *barrios*. Men would always accuse *me* of wanting *them*; they would rarely admit *they* wanted me – *Eso si que es ser maricón. ¿Qué dice usted?* I grasped that whatever was to happen would always be in secret, hidden from people, hidden from the *varón* himself, and I would have to fabricate and sustain most of the seduction, initially at least. When I was thirteen I began to receive a more formal carnal education from the old priest who ran my school summer camp. I found solace and warmth in his benign soft-textured body and in his pleasant ways, not too condescending, kindhearted but not too vulnerable, always making judicious use of the authority dispensed by God. He taught me how to

genuflect and showed me that love hurts only if you're not giving
yourself completely to it. Once one is blinded by its shining light
there is no need to hide, there is nowhere to hide. It was only then
that the *santa misa* began to make sense to me.

The gentle pedagogy of this old priest was abruptly disrupted some
years later when I met Gabriel, a blinding buck who was doing his
military service in a navy regiment in Valparaiso; his pants and shirts
were crisply pressed against his skin, and his belt perfectly coiled
around his narrow waist. The day I met him he had come to Santiago
on furlough. It was his first time in the city, poor guy, to think he
would end up being ambushed by my desire! Like many other young
soldiers at that time, he walked around the downtown area searching
for action, any action, without a clear idea of what it would look like
except that it involved getting his rocks off.

He did not respond well to me when I approached him in the *por-
tales* of *Plaza de Armas.* "Are you fucking crazy?" he barked and I
thought he would hit me. I had followed him for an hour and had
crossed the boulevard after him, stopping when he paused in front of a
store window, picking up the pace when he would almost get lost
among the herds of pedestrians. "You fucking queer!" he added. I just
smiled. Half an hour later, I caught up with him at the *Parque Forestal*
near the *Museo de Bellas Artes.* I was standing a few steps behind him
and he suddenly turned to face me, marched right up to me with sure
footing, and grabbed me by the neck, his breath on my face like the
spring wind of September.

"You know what we do to queers in the navy?" Gabriel showed
me a clenched fist.

"Show me," I muttered.

"Fuck you!" He let go of my neck. "How old are you, anyway?"

"Old enough to make you feel good." The rest, as the say, is history.

Gabriel was twenty-one and I was fifteen, but – I am telling you – it was I who passed on to Gabriel everything the priest had carefully taught me and then some. After a few visits to Santiago on weekends, I had him hooked and he came back for more. Whenever he paused, maybe entertaining some anxious doubts, I would pull him back with the careful mesh of my words: *yo soy y seré siempre como la hembra y eso no te hace a ti sino el varón*. I would reassure him how he had seduced me, how in love I was, how I couldn't live without him, and Gabriel, the navy angel, would resume his explorations with gusto. *¿Quién lo va a saber, si tus labios me desean, y te juntas con mi piel?* I carefully reprised the lines of every afternoon *radioteatro* that my mother and I had listened to on the transistor while she ironed and starched end-less piles of humid clothes or polished silver cutlery. It was a dream world of serpentine melodrama filled with advice on domestic prob-lems, drunk abusive boyfriends, impotent two-timing lovers, too old or too inhibited by their size, their religious stupidity, or their moth-ers, advice exchanged across the high wrought-iron fences that sur-rounded the mansions while the maids were watering the manicured lawns and flowerbeds. *Yo soy la orquídea inmaculada que asemeja a la hem-bra y en su centro, en mis entrañas no hay sino candor como materia preciosa y la fertilidad que te ofrezco en el vaivén de mi danza.* I wasn't embarrassed to repeat these lines, words, and images in Gabriel's gullible ears. He concealed his pleasure at hearing them, but the beating of his organs and the hardening of his body always gave him away.

Gabriel and I gradually enacted every foolish adolescent fantasy. No fruit I had ever savoured before had tasted this strange, wild, and good. When Gabriel discovered that I had a devoted thing going on the side with a priest, he went mad. He beat the shit out of me, and then he went and threatened the priest with scandal and injury if he didn't stop seeing me. The priest scurried away like a church rat. When my mother saw the signs of my involvement with Gabriel, she sighed. I guess she was comforted by the thought that I wouldn't become a man of the cloth. For her, Gabriel looked like a real man, therefore, under his influence, I couldn't be any more of a flaming flower than I already was. I didn't have a father, so this association with a young man in uniform could only help, right?

THREE YEARS AFTER GABRIEL HAD GIVEN UP HIS dreams of staying in the navy, he had broken up with his girlfriend back in his hometown and was working odd jobs in Santiago to support himself and Camilo. They had started their liaison right around the time that Camilo was thrown out from the Jewish household where his mother worked when he was caught indulging with the young man of the house, just before Yom Kippur, no less. The young men moved into in a miserable room they rented in the tough *Calle Carmen*, a decrepit adobe house they shared with the smoking landlady. Theirs was always a passionate and intractable relationship; many evenings they would turn up at *El Goce Pagano* to drink beer and often got into a jealous brawl that they would take home and, amidst yells and broken glasses, end by having rowdy sex late into the night. In the adjacent room, the landlady, who turned occasional tricks, would knock hard on the wall so they would stop the racket. They would make love again in the morning before Gabriel went to work and Camilo went to the *liceo*. It was hard to make ends meet and Camilo was restless, so after school, when Gabriel was at work, he would go out and meet other men. When Gabriel asked him where the extra money was coming from, Camilo said that it was from his mother or from friends. They would use the cash to buy groceries, glossy magazines, beer, or clothing.

Things began to change when Camilo finished high school at seventeen and received a high enough score on the national examinations to choose a career in the humanities. He decided to be a teacher. A new horizon began to open in Camilo's mind during that first year at the *Universidad de Santiago*, a horizon that included a new kind of man. Gabriel grew jealous and resentful of his lover's intellectual airs, and his long absences in the evenings to study with who he saw as arrogant classmates. Their domestic life became even more despairing and their sex even more torrid. One morning, bruised and exhausted after one of those tortuous nights, Camilo took his books and clothes and left Gabriel. First, he knocked at Italo's door; he had recently met him at a political rally at the university. Italo had no qualms in admitting that he was no *comunista indecente*, but was attending with the express purpose of seducing an old but affluent Marxist professor. When Italo turned him down with various excuses, Camilo went to Cesar, whom he had met in the street one evening when Camilo was getting out of a stranger's car, some fresh cash burning in his pocket. Cesar, in the blunt manner that he would cultivate his entire life, told Camilo he would ask his father if he could stay in his house if Camilo agreed to tone down his clothes, speech, and manners to a level worthy of *la gente decente* and would be fully truthful about his background. Cesar lived with his patriarchal father and a slew of straight-laced siblings in a big *Nuñoa* 1920s house on *Calle Bilbao*, a maze of whimsical corridors and portholes far from the ratty downtown core. Camilo immediately agreed to these conditions because he had no place to go and had intuitively trusted Cesar's innate wisdom since their first meeting when, seeing him step out of the rich man's car, he had come up to Camilo and told him point blank, "That is no sugar daddy. That is a rich sonnovabitch who always picks up chickens and gives them the clap." "*Una cosa es ser puta, y loca del culo,*" Cesar explained his philosophy unequivocally, "*pero otra muy diferente es ser loca de la cabeza, mi linda.*" Even as young as he was then, Cesar heckled like an uptown matron, but his wisdom was as solid as his dignity and pride.

Gabriel was incensed and looked for him everywhere. Someone warned Camilo that he was "packing heat," as they say in English. He knew that Camilo wasn't one to stay home on sacred Saturday night.

Gabriel systematically made the rounds of the few existing clandestine gay night clubs, and finally caught up with Camilo at *El Fausto* on *Avenida Santa Maria*, a pricey night club where the "A" list faggotry of the town gathered to discuss their latest lovers, their travels to Europe, and fashion trends. The place was clandestine but ignored by corrupted local authorities. Cesar, of course, would have none of Camilo's taste for *El Goce Pagano* and judiciously dragged him to what he called "a place where decent people meet." Gabriel busting Camilo at *El Fausto* was a brief scene, but it quickly made the rounds in this milieu. Camilo barely had time to react before being turned around by a sonorous slap in the face, the blaring disco music muffling the sound, but before he could slip away under a table or through a back door, he was pulled outside by the hair, pounded on the front sidewalk, and recriminated sourly for his betrayals. Then Gabriel hailed a cab, pushed Camilo in, and instructed the driver to speed them to the *Calle Carmen* address. This kind of thing happened frequently and Camilo took the beatings and the scenes, but he had made up his mind and never fully went back to Gabriel. He would go back to Gabriel's room and stay some nights, like a person who is slowly paying a debt or has put his freedom in a layaway plan. At the end of Camilo's eventful first university year, Gabriel seemed to give up; he moved away from the *Calle Carmen* address, promising never to relinquish ownership of Camilo's heart and ass, and Camilo went back to live there. Gradually Camilo's suitors became more upscale – painters, teachers, engineers – until he had one for each day of the week – he was wined and dined by them, got a bit of cash to get by, as well as his share of diseases. He cemented his friendships with Cesar, Mariana Nomeolvides, and even with the disdainful Italo. From each person that crossed his path he absorbed everything he could – manners, sexual appetite, and taste – the stuff that makes *la gente decente* – decent people.

ANDREW AND I SHARED ONE THOUSAND AND ONE stories during those winter days and nights. What else is friendship but a constant telling? I won the heart of a friend by telling my life away, naming the names of others and their stories – the legendary Chela, the tempestuous Gabriel, my mothers, the priests, the protesters, and the soldiers. It seemed that I had come to a standstill and there was not much more to live for. And, in between the few times that Andrew and I could steal away together, there was silence and rain, trickling memories – *I can't stand the rain / against my window / reaching down like bitter memories / llueve / tras de los cristales, llueve y llueve.* These lines echo in my mind.

This morning, I watched the rain pouring outside for hours. I take a good look at myself in a mirror and put together the composite of a healthy young man, exhuming memories, caressing the few unscathed patches of skin. Why do we get sick? Who is to blame for this? It would be so much easier if there really were a patient zero, a guilty victim, one closeted gay traitor to blame, or the African monkeys, a CIA conspiracy against homosexuals, *Latinos*, and blacks. It would be easier if the chemical help had arrived earlier for some of us. It would be easier if people out there didn't fool themselves by thinking that there is a cure. What cure can there be for the contagion of sex between males? It is destined to be a lethal alchemy, and I say this with no prejudice. I wouldn't have it any other way. Give me the venom of the male sperm anytime over the placid life of the abstinent. Give me the drudgery of decaying health over the untouched skin that has never suffered the abrasions of heated love. If I can't belong to the North America Olympus reserved for the beautiful and the bold, the rich and the famous, at least I can join the ranks of the mediocre brothers and sisters to the stars: the victims. I refuse to be one who only gazes at the stars and martyrs in tabloids and talk shows. Who writes as I speak? There is always a lovely and gentle hand that writes as I reminisce with little rhyme or reason, opening and closing doors to recollections I didn't think I had, like the time when Roger opened his own door and crossed his threshold, two months after my surgery, and we stood face to face, surprised – for a fleeting instant we couldn't recognize each other. We were strangers.

THE SLOW PACE OF THE HOUSEHOLD CHANGED noticeably as soon as Roger came back. There was always something to do, to see, to shop for; there were people to entertain, Roger's kids would come every weekend, and the telephone never stopped ringing off the hook. Roger spoke in carefully calibrated words − the voice of the master − and Camilo listened to him with perky ears like the RCA dog. He took a special interest − like one embarking on a home improvement project − in Camilo's studies at the university, he wanted to see what he wrote and to discuss all his ideas, although he rarely agreed with the ways Camilo took to produce his thinking and much less with his opinions once formulated. Roger was an acid critic of Camilo's stream-of-consciousness prose. He said that as a teacher he couldn't stand the idea of having someone messing around with structures and meanings. He aligned Camilo's words, placing commas like someone inserts hard wedges to strengthen a dam, cutting sentences and paragraphs with architectural precision. Camilo complained that these changes pruned his imagination, his curiosity and passion, and made his writing spastic and truncated, full of stops and abbreviations. He said he preferred the sinuous fabric of Spanish crawling through the desert of blank pages. Roger, who had said he would learn Spanish, said that was absurd. When things between them would come to an impasse, Roger would pragmatically suggest that they have sex, where he also had much to instruct.

ROGER WAS AN ARIES, A PATRIARCH WITH A FIRM command on the reins of his chariot. He would never act in excess, and his extravagant spending was framed in the most logical rationale so it would make sense to everyone. I am a Pisces, contradictory, spiritual, given to hedonism and comfort. I prefer sentiment to sex, erotic fantasy to bodily performance. Roger's unquenchable thirst for sex absorbed a great portion of my stamina. If I became tired after forty-five minutes or so and let my body just hang there, he would adjust it to a new and implausible position to keep his sexual machinery going. It is not that I didn't enjoy his voracious appetite, his requests, or his demands for versatility and flexibility, but I was stunned by his rigidity in setting schedules and his perseverance in following them to the tee. I realized that this wasn't necessarily an idiosyncratic trait, it had something to do with the infamous Protestant work ethic. One is to work seriously, fuck seriously, and have fun . . . seriously.

Okay, I wasn't innocent. I excuse ignorance but I abhor innocence. I sure knew what I was doing. I provided the flavour to our relationship; Roger's acquaintances made patronizing remarks about how young and exotic I was. I was the one with unexpected yet charming reactions, the one who was puzzling and amusing. I was scary but sexy, but if I challenged them on their condescending titillation, they would back right off. In fact, it was our sex, not our intellect that made Roger and I different. I preferred to acquire a new taste, I sought the contrast of something chilled and viscous in my taste buds, or something sizzling and crusty, things that I could approach timidly. I liked getting to know the flesh of man before devouring it. I liked to be at once the hunter and the prey. Roger was a carnivorous and swift animal. He often seemed to have another, more important, task to take on soon after. However, I insist I wasn't innocent, and during our first year together, it was a thrill to be part of Roger's sexual theatre. I appreciated the time he would take to audition our cast of characters, the explicitness with which we were all to deliver our sparse lines. You can take the boy out of the church, but you can't take the Catholic pageantry out of the boy, something about his Spartan scenarios made me feel inadequate, almost prudish. In any case I felt I just couldn't say no, so I didn't, even when I wasn't particularly attracted to the scenes or the actors. Roger's insatiable energy and great skill intrigued me deeply, but I began to see that he operated on technique, not intuition. I became his willing accomplice. We started to go to a seedy bathhouse downtown, labyrinthine and filthy, filled with cubicles with no doors, and we would end in a pile of limbs. The smell of the worked-up bodies would always turn my reticence into raw lust. I'd go into some kind of frenzy, my eyes dilated, panting, searching for the next organ, the next vibration, and the next orgasm. The best fuck of the night was always to come later. I could hear disapproving voices talking about addiction, compulsion, and low self-esteem. If only it were that easy to explain.

Between the walls of the house on Pender Street I gradually began to experience withdrawals, *cortocircuitos*, the slippage of words, pools of silence, strange permutations between languages. I neglected to write the accents in Spanish words in my letters to Chela and she scolded me for it. I didn't think aloud or curse in Spanish. English was ubiquitous, I couldn't get rid of it, and sometimes I felt gagged by it. It was there day and night, in bed, in sex, on television, in the medicine cabinet, in recipes, in the dictionaries and listings, tattooed on everything. It even seemed to cancel out the French printed underneath. One day my anxious musings crystallized into one realization: I was scared to die feeling like a foreigner. Roger would be there for me, but the thought of getting sick and having him or anyone earnestly run every aspect of my existence made me uneasy for the first time. I needed to return to Chile and repossess the things that had once belonged to me: the crowded streets, the buildings, the pollution, the noise, the dilapidated public places, the dark and sheltering parks, and the thrilling nightlife I missed so much. It had taken me so long to begin to shed some of the nostalgia, to convince myself that I would one day fully belong in Canada. I was afraid of upsetting this fragile balance. Just as I had tried to erase the sediment of those deep-seated Catholic beliefs, I tried to obliterate everything that was *Latino*, but I couldn't. It was like a phantom limb, a piece of me nagging somewhere inside my flesh, hurting from time to time. I tried to explain all these experiences in several letters to Chela, to put in plain words how Roger's firm grip over the reins of the household and what happened under that roof made me feel: contradictory, uneasy, inadequate, and incomplete. Often I felt more like a suburban trophy wife who dispenses smiles while elevating her well-heeled legs than like an intrepid *Latino* queen. One day, after I had typed and printed a brief and cryptic note – whereas before I would have mailed a lovely handwritten card – and when folding the crisp white sheet, I realized that I had written it entirely in English. I tore it up and started a new one.

ONE EVENING, AFTER A TRYING DAY THAT HAD left Camilo's nerves raw, Roger had responded with his austere silence, and things seemed to come to a head as Camilo was slicing the roast for dinner. They had not talked much for days. It was long after a few terse words were exchanged that Camilo wielded the kitchen knife right in front of Roger's wincing eyes.

"All I'm saying is that I need to go back to Chile, if only to see, to make sure it is still there," Camilo blurted out.

"Camilo, I can't keep up with your sudden mood swings and outbursts. They are irrational, childish, and unproductive. If you're trying to manipulate me with them, you're being unsuccessful." A couple of months earlier Roger had said that he didn't mind a little manipulation at all. He had gone as far as to say that he thought it was charming.

"I can't understand how you switch on and off, get hard, get off, socialize, have dinner, keep on working at your desk," Camilo continued. "I feel I need to be myself, go to Chile . . . I don't know."

Roger was unmoved. "I fail to see how your behaviour bears any relationship to wanting to go to Chile." Camilo was straight-jacketed by his impeccably linear thinking.

"I'm scared, I'm being swallowed by you, losing my roots. I feel like a fucking human Bonsai – worse, you treat me like a housewife, even when I am like a whore, it's weird, it is . . . oppressing."

"Your attempts to be feminist and politically correct are preposterous." Roger switched to a professorial tone. "Oppressing? Save the buzzwords for your essays. You can't self-righteously accuse anyone of oppression, racism, homophobia, or misogyny at the drop of a hat. And, can you keep it down please?" As Camilo relaxed his trembling hand and lay the knife down, Roger added, "There is no need for histrionics. Now, *there* is a good word for you."

"It is the way I feel," Camilo, humiliated, muttered as his eyes welled up. He started to pace energetically around the kitchen.

"And yet you claim oppression." Roger coldly jabbed him with these words. "It requires a degree of rationality on your part, don't you think? Maybe you should look the word oppression up in a dictionary."

Camilo's voice rose an octave. "Shove the dictionary up your ass. God knows bigger things go that way. I'm fucking talking about how *you* fucking make *me* feel."

"Enough! If you feel like a housewife, it's because maybe you act like one. I will refrain from treating you as such if you refrain from acting effeminately." Roger's countenance had changed, he was angry now, but his voice remained harsh and low. He had carefully pushed the kitchen door shut so the guest in the other room, a man decked in leather who had been invited to dinner and sex, could not hear. "You often act giddy, flippant like a high school girl. It is inappropriate behaviour. If you do *not* monitor your unearned sarcasm, it will hinder your academic potential." Roger delivered the lines like a diagnosis.

"Oh yeah? It'll come back to bite me in the ass? I'm too queer! This is what you're saying? You're fucking afraid the guy in the other room will not want to fuck with us tonight because I am too flaming! Worse, you're afraid people at the university will figure out that you and I are lovers. Well, fuck you!"

"Don't be ridiculous . . . and, there is no need to curse."

"If you're a fag, you should go all the way, man! Not halfway there. Your shit about behaviour sounds to me like a big fucking closet." Camilo was close to Roger's face, prodding, seeking a reaction he could recognize and knew he could manage, but it did not come. Roger was in absolute control of himself.

Roger shrugged his shoulders. "That's all in the past. You're in Canada now. You're protected. Now, you can read and write about oppression. Be rational." Having said this, he slowly turned around and exited the kitchen. Camilo heard Roger apologize to the leather-clad stranger in the other room and he followed him.

"Fuck you!" Camilo yelled. Pointing an irate finger at the tall stranger who had started to leave, he added, "And fuck you too! Your fucking rationality only works if you don't behave like a fag. Don't ask, don't tell. Same shit, different country, different closet." Roger and the leather stranger were stumped by this sudden shift in focus, but Camilo had more to say. "How come they don't play slow music in bars here? So fags don't touch each other in public, that's why." No one had flesh that night, neither for dinner nor for dessert.

Camilo began to plan his homecoming to Chile and spent hours on the phone talking with Cesar, Andrew, and Sol. Roger remained silently civil. He still brought strangers over to feast on sex, and although he politely invited Camilo to join them, he would make no effort in having Camilo participate. Camilo's guard went up the day that Roger dragged someone named Joseph in from some peep show on Granville Street, a thirty-something dropout philosophy student on Prozac, and kept him flat on his face for an entire weekend. Joseph was beautiful, like an alabaster reproduction of a Greek idol, with a permanent expression of divine thoughtfulness on his face, and his sexual stoicism inspired Roger. Soon after that first weekend, Joseph returned and stayed over some nights, and then for three entire days. When Roger was at work at the university and Camilo attending classes, Joseph was given free rein to exercise his compulsion for cleaning, cooking, and gardening.

I TRIED TO FIGURE OUT WHAT WAS GOING ON. About a month into this threesome, I tried to fuck Joseph on the side to see whether that would put my inner troubles to rest. It didn't work. Guided by his unfathomable rationality, Roger sat us both down and, without a trace of irony, explained his theory about gay men not being tied up by the emotional trappings of heterosexuality, that we could share our beds and our household with love and respect. It sounded like arrested flower-power to me, but framed with Protestant austerity. He sounded like one of those Jonestown freaks who begins a cult of many wives and isolated lives. Joseph would move in temporarily while I was in Chile. I was about to be dethroned by a passive creature who fastidiously dusted as he proffered philosophic edicts! No, not me! That was la *gota que derramó el vaso*, I could tolerate the ghost of Roger's former lover, his spoiled son and daughter trampling around the house on weekends, the muffled condescension of his university associates, his domestic and petty tyranny, but Joseph wedging his way into my territory pushed me over the edge.

Next thing I knew I had blood on my knuckles. Ah! Those precious and reliable male hormones. I was squeezing his throat when Roger and his son came running down the stairs. They had a hard time snatching Joseph, the prophet of doom, away from my claws. Then I went berserk. They looked for cover against the wall. I broke a couple of windows, hurled a few ashtrays across the room. I thought later that this was a bit more *Fatal Attraction* than the incident with the knife, but I was deep into it before I could think. I looked at Joseph. "You'd better get your sorry white ass out of here if you value your fucking depressing life. Now!" I pointed a trembling finger at Roger. "You *gringo de mierda*. How dare you do this to me?" Everybody chilled. I couldn't think of anything else to say, so I stormed out of the place. I ran all over town crying, too embarrassed to go and find shelter at Andrew's or Sol's. Yes, they had "told me so," but I didn't need to hear it again.

I did so much agitated thinking on those few days I ran away from Roger's house and wandered around Vancouver. I stayed nights in the local bathhouses, falling asleep to the drone of the endless beat of the music, "slave to the rhythm" as Miss Grace Jones would repeat again and again, and I spent whatever little money I had to buy some food and to drink. I have never felt the way I felt then, so terribly alien to this Canadian land, to my existence here, and to my own skin. I questioned everything, and the few answers I got were painful little pearls of wisdom – like pulling out one's own teeth. I kept on wondering what Chile was, and what I had left behind in what now seemed like an eternity ago. I wondered, "Is it a tropical island like everybody seems to believe? Is it *tropicalisimo, caliente,* of *salsa* lessons and spicy cookbooks, *la bamba, la rumba, andale, andale, arriba, arriba,* and all that Tex-Mex bullshit people say when I tell them I'm *Latino*?" I reviewed the lessons I had learned so far: to be *Latino* is to be somebody else's liquid dream, spicy as *jalapeños*, sexual and basic. It is impossible to be Canadian, it is impossible *not* to be different in a country that cannot have one unified identity, that is inhabited by orphans, exiles, and accidental offspring; a country that suffers everyday not to get more and more mixed up – although such is its destiny. A country that refuses to admit that it is awfully young and inexperienced, always in the shadow of the overblown, testosterone-filled icon of its neighbour, always comparing penises – who has the biggest? – always comparing everything, but often coming in second and thus feeling inadequate – Canada possesses a *mestizo* soul trapped in the pristine body of a developed country. I felt I was suffering similar growing pains. I looked at myself in the mirrors of the eyes of those around me and I hated my new adolescence, a phase that didn't seem to be about to wear out any time soon.

Still, here I am – even today. There is no real country beyond the border. It's a mirage, effective advertising for thirsty postmodern drivers putting in 5K on an arid, frozen, and deserted highway – *una hembra curvilínea y neumática de calendario de taller mecánico, de comercial de cerveza en la tele,* a Camel-smoking *un Habano* in a white linen suit and panama hat, *vendiendo flamantes* Cadillacs *con diente brillante de oro, con abultado bolsillo y abultada entrepierna,* or selling weekend packages in *Cancún* and *Varadero.* Yet I know that the people I describe are real and not just nostalgic shrines – *las animitas* – that one finds in front yards or on winding roads in Chile, surrounded by halos of candles that mark the place where someone was run over by a car in the pitch dark of the night. Now the whirlwind of questions seems to have slowed down. Now the languages seem to thread together into a common yarn with more ease – *se enhebran los lenguajes con la tranquilidad con que uno enhebra los dedos en el pelo del amado en el atardecer.* In English, I recount the years I have lived in Canada, illness, contagion, the perils of sex and love in a strange and cold ecology, small afflictions and indignities that trickle down on me, piercing my skin like needles in a diabolic acupuncture. *En español, yo hablo de la ternura y la seducción.* I have always been, and I will always be, obscene, promiscuous, and my tongue, like the serpent, will always be sliced in two. I will make love to the eardrum and the rosy anus of *gringos,* and I will bite hard the nipples of the *moreno* chest of my *Latinos.* I have fallen in love with both worlds and in both ways, sexually stereophonic, I can receive and understand affection and derision in both my official tongues. Someone comes to my bedside to soothe my fever and calm me down, the voice says that I should try to rest, not speak too much. But, I can't help it, I am joyous, the days I feel better and the homemaker or the street nurse is here, I tell stories. Do I *ever* tell stories — *una serpentina de palabras y recuerdos.* I can hear my words take shape, stumble on each other like toddlers and take flight in spirals.

CAMILO RETURNED TO THE HOUSE AFTER A FEW days. It was after midnight. He slowly walked upstairs. Roger was watching television and didn't acknowledge his presence at the top of the stairs. There was no trace of the philosopher. The heavy silence was amplified by the incessant trickling of the cold rain outside. Camilo begged Roger to forgive him. He said it quietly and fully. Roger remained expressionless as the young man recited promises to behave rationally one-by-one in an emotional *hara-kiri*. He promised he would partic- ipate joyfully in Roger's sexual games, he said he enjoyed them but that he was going through "a phase," and that he would harness his temper, his foolish jealousy, his mannerisms and attire, and find new ways to satisfy him. He asked Roger to help him exorcise his anger. He said he could write it down, a promissory note, a truce, a recapitulation on his part. After a prolonged silence Roger stood up, walked over to Camilo, and, towering over him, grabbed his chin in the strong palm of his hand, checked his reddened eyes, and pushed him away to walk downstairs into the basement without uttering a word. Camilo walked behind him, still crying.

"I can't comprehend why you want it to be like this." Roger's voice was steely. "How do I know this won't happen again?"

"Make me remember my promise." There was an odd glint in Camilo's eyes as he took his damp clothes off. He knelt down and unfastened Roger's belt. He made it sibilate like a blade being drawn out of its sheath and presented it to him. Roger branded, blow by blow, the terms of their contract on his cold skin, not a single moan escaping Camilo's lips, even as the lashes gradually increased in rhythm and vigor. Once the flesh had been atoned, on the bare floor, in silence Roger entered him. Only then Camilo cried and thanked him and whispered the last Spanish words his lips would utter while under that roof: "*Señor, no soy digno de entrar en tu casa, pero una palabra tuya bastará para sanarme.*" There was a warm streak on his lips and a forest of flames up his back.

I DIDN'T GO BACK TO CHILE. CESAR WAS frustrated, angry, and saddened by this, but he went anyway. Juan couldn't go with him because he had been unable to get his legal papers. He was trying a different lawyer in Miami, but she was taking her sweet time, not to mention his money. Being the eternal optimist that he was, he kept on trying. He said that Mariana Nomeolvides and her dubious contacts would be of more help this time, but I told him to be careful, she was full of shit. Of all places in the world, I found a part-time job as an interpreter at the immigration department. What else can a foreigner do but speak his own fucking language! I heard amazing stories of tortured and humiliated refugees, heard asinine lies, and I had the responsibility of conveying them truthfully, but in the best possible light. I cringed every morning when we – lawyers, refugees, and small bureaucrats – demurely paraded into the hearing room, waiting for the members of the refugee board, possessed with grace and temperance, to appear through a different door, and went through the circumspect, time-consuming, and absurd protocol. This was the backstage of Canada's sanctuary, *no todo lo que brilla es oro*, populated by the arrogance of lawyers, their heavy-handed stereotyping, their pity and disdain masquerading as concern. The stilted theatre of multiculturalism. I could only wish that once these newcomers went through this ordeal they wouldn't hate us all too much, that they would be able to find their way in the over-regulated Canadian reality out there.

At that time, I wrote a long letter to Chela, explaining myself. Now that I read it again I find it almost telegraphic.

"*Diosa*: No, I'm not coming to Santiago. I know you wanted me there so much, I promised, *pero la vida es una tom-tom-tómbola*, I have decided that this isn't the best time. Since the incident with that fucking philosopher I have been trying to patch things up, yes, sometimes it is like you and Uli, sometimes it feels like a vicious circle. I have almost finished the classes I need to get my degree and I have applied to do graduate work in the same faculty where Roger teaches. He suggested it, I think he wanted to prove he wasn't scared of his colleagues finding out we live together, that we are not just 'friends.' He didn't say so, but I know. My other news might sound weird – we are going to Europe, yes, all over the place! I wish it had been at another time but I never *en mi puta vida* dreamed of going to Europe. I am so excited, I feel like a fucking Evita."

I didn't tell Chela about the other stuff, our strange sexual life. I didn't write to her about a couple of nights before Roger and I left for England when I made a clandestine excursion to a bathhouse. Roger had taken his daughter, son, and ex-wife out for dinner. I think they wanted to talk about money in private. I was at odds with my thoughts, didn't know whether I was excited or pissed about this expedition to Europe. It felt like a consolation prize. Any other time it would have been a dream come true. Not then. Sitting in a small dark cubicle of the bathhouse I was lost in my thoughts when a small face with gloomy, burrowed eyes and paint-brush eyebrows came my way and *en menos de lo que canta un gallo* we were embroiled in a savage fuck. The stout man mounted me vigorously, broke two condoms, and replaced them amidst loud huffs, then he gnawed at my neck, and gripped my nipples with fury. When our spent bodies separated; the stranger wanted to talk. I was sore and spaced out, wondering how I would cover the bruises all over my body and the pain in my asshole, but we got into a conversation. He told me he was an AIDS activist on the Downtown East Side, the eyesore of pristine Vancouver; his eagerness made me smile, a Trotskyite, ugly as sin, offbeat, intense. I was redeemed in his eyes because I was an offspring of the working class who had grown up in a dictatorship – though the story was getting a bit stale for me. He was a cross between Hitler and Chaplin – both, I'm told, were sexually quite potent – and he had the deranged eyes of Little Richard. He told me about being a "queer" in "mainstream politics," a mouthful of new words, and how liberals are tolerant on the outside but didn't really accept homosexuals outside those boundaries. It made me think. He told me I should do something instead of sitting on my ass. (Why is someone always giving me advice on ass management?) I should write about social change. He reminded me of my fellow Chilean university classmates and their inflammatory political rhetoric. However, I found his ideas a refreshing break from the white-picket fence atmosphere that surrounded our bawdy house on Pender Street. I wasn't about to become a revolutionary guerrilla sister, but I promised myself I would learn more about politics and community and all those things. I knew I would see this ugly Trotskyite again.

CHELA HAD PHONED THE NIGHT BEFORE THEY left Vancouver, cackled a terse hello to Roger, and asked to talk with Camilo. She was calling to tell him he must not leave London without first looking for Ramiro, an alias, a Chilean who lived there, who had met Chela before "the change," and they had become good friends. In hushed tones, Chela explained that she had helped this Ramiro character when he was in hiding in *La Serena*, the *Norte Chico* town that Uli was from, and Chela had been instrumental in getting Ramiro some papers so he could cross the Andes to Argentina and from there fly to Europe. Camilo was surprised to know that Chela had ever set foot in *La Serena* but when he interrupted Chela to ask her to explain this visit, Chela curtly answered that she was "taking care of business" at that time and that she did not want to pursue this tangent. Camilo had to hear the rest of Ramiro's story; he had belonged to the *Movimiento de Izquierda Revolucionaria*, a longstanding armed group of the radical left. During the 1980s' wave of military repression, Ramiro had fled Chile to escape sure death at the hands of the CNI, the Chilean secret police who had targeted him as a communist terrorist. He had been incarcerated and tortured. He entered Germany illegally, and later moved to England where he married an English woman under a new name to get his residency. During his years of clandestine living, Ramiro realized what the party had made him deny: that he liked communist boys, not girls. Chela was one of the few people on earth who knew his real name and history, but she would not tell Camilo any more details — "*El que nada sabe nada teme,*" she added in a doomsayer's tone. When Camilo proffered this news to Roger, he left out various details. Roger didn't ask any questions, absorbed as he was in grading his students at the last minute and thoroughly planning their European tour.

 ROGER RAN A TIGHT SHIP, A WHIRLWIND OF PRE-planned activities where I had an allocated spot. Almost upon departure, a strange numbness took over. It was clear that I was to follow and enjoy myself where designated. All I remember of the first days is feeling overwhelmed by an overload of stimuli. We stayed at the Philbeach Hotel in Earls Court. Once I could free myself from our schedule, I looked for Ramiro, knowing well the potential fiasco of meeting compatriots outside Chile. I had met enough Chileans in Vancouver. I didn't trust them and they disapproved of my "lifestyle." I found him and his lover in a decrepit room they rented in a house close to East Finchley Station, where they kept on feeding coins into a hopeless heater. He didn't look anything like I imagined terrorists to be. Ramiro was friendly, caring, a big guy with clumsy gestures who in a garbled British accent kept saying "Lovely, lovely!" to everything I said. We had a great afternoon, we clicked as they say, and our conversation flowed easily. When I went back to the hotel after our first encounter, I was radiant. I told Roger about Ramiro, though not everything. He stated dispassionately that he understood the hard life of immigrants because fifteen years ago he had been an American immigrant in Canada. I thought moving from Illinois (or was it Ohio?) to British Columbia was hardly comparable to moving across the ocean to England or across the continent to Canada bearing an accent, *moreno* skin, and a murky political past, but I didn't say anything. I went back to visit Ramiro several times, when I could take time off from my marital duties. Roger didn't protest; he didn't seem to care as long as we made our scheduled visits to tourist attractions – so much stolen stuff they have packed in those museums! – and as long as I was back at the hotel at night to engage in his games with all sorts of pasty white boys with thick English accents I barely understood. One of the times I headed to Finchley Station, Ramiro took

me to his booth in Camden Town where he sold handicrafts, and dope under the table. There, retreated under a makeshift plastic awning, our feet drenched in rain and our hands quivering, we sat for hours, smoking, people-watching, and talking about all those years of living away from home. From time to time we would leave Ramiro's lanky punk lover in charge of the stall to run through the pouring rain to a greasy pub nearby to get cigarettes, beer, and cheap, greasy Indian food that we would bring back in heavy brown paper bags. One night Roger, reluctantly, allowed me to stay with Ramiro. However, he never expressed any interest in meeting him. Ramiro and his lover took me to some sort of underground party – a rave, he called it – and before going in a dark alley back door, we popped a couple of pills. Inside, the smoky warehouse was chock full of shirtless skinheads, as Ramiro called them, they looked like punks to me, but apparently that was not "in" anymore. How many hours we spent there, I couldn't count; all I remember is letting my body slip into a dance trance that felt like one grandiose communal fuck. A couple of days after that fabulous night, Roger and I left London.

Roger and I kept a polite silence during that trip. We never disagreed and I never got too excited about anything, not even sex with strangers; this I interpreted as a triumph over my emotions. We made all the stops scheduled on Roger's itinerary. Our next stop was *el Barrio Gotic* in Barcelona where we stayed at the house of an artist Roger had met on a previous trip, who lived on *el Carrer De L'hopital* near *Las Ramblas*. He was an alcoholic painter of thick smeared red and yellow strokes. In between half-filled glasses of liquor, Roger alternatively fucked him mercilessly and counseled him about relationships for three days. It struck me how Roger so intently surrounded himself with what he called "productive" and "creative" people and how he went about it in the same deliberate way in which one puts place cards on a table for a dinner party. I didn't think that this guy's art was very good – what the fuck do I know about art anyway? Sebastian was his name. I know that Sebastian was somewhat true to his name and had various rashes on his torso that he carefully covered while having sex with us. I was reluctant – I felt like that a lot those days – but I went along with it. I think Sebastian was the first man with AIDS I ever saw. If I learned something from Roger, it was not to flinch before any physical difference. He was an equal opportunity whore; no scar, wound, or birth defect would deter Roger from savouring a man's flesh – there's something positive to be said about *that*.

Then we went on to Madrid and later Toledo, and just about then the trip turned into a quickly edited diorama, some sort of video clip: Goya paintings, Antoni Gaudi buildings, *tapas*, deafening traffic, monumental churches full of Japanese tourists, flash! flash! flash! *la Puerta del Sol, la Puerta de Alcalá*. . . . After weeks in Spain we hopped over to Amsterdam where for the first two weeks we hardly saw the light of day, so dedicated were we to the night leather scene; I remember more about barking like a dog in the slippery basement of the Argos and other bars on the *Warmoesstraat* than visiting Anne Frank's house. However, when I took to going for walks alone and discovered the weed stores and their potent products, I found an enormous solace in the city's austere spaces. Anything was a solace after the sheer madness of Madrid and Barcelona. My silly Catholic beliefs had made it difficult to enjoy this delightful habit before. While wandering the lovely narrow streets of Amsterdam by myself, I was overtaken by an easygoing optimism that went to my head like champagne bubbles, and it allowed me to fully dedicate my senses to this delightful pastime. When I had half a chance to talk to some of those attractive, yet stern-looking, portly leather Dutch men, instead of getting fucked or smacked around by them, I enjoyed them tremendously – sisters will be sisters, always, under the same ray of sunlight.

Being in Europe with my New World Svengali wasn't completely negative. I was learning something reassuring about my body and myself. I had more than one offer to leave it all behind and stay, but I declined, always wondering why I was being so stubborn, always wondering why one has to go back to places that are not particularly lovable or inhabitable, but that strangely feel like home. One sweet, thin man in *Baños El Condal* in Barcelona had offered to elope with me to Paris. I turned him down, I was probably terrified that he would reject me if he knew I was positive – mind you, he looked in rough shape himself and he had not used a condom. I saw very few men on that European trek ask for a condom; it was as if the plague had not touched Europe. By the time we arrived in Amsterdam I had revived my old Catholic habit of modesty and went on sexual expeditions alone in the times that Roger didn't require my presence – a modicum of modesty is defensible. In Amsterdam, a sweet giant named Jan I met at Thermos-by-Day bathhouse also offered a quiet life of books and spacious interiors, not to mention a sizable pound of leather-clad flesh and muscles, and a wad of cash. Once again, such an offer made me feel beautiful and intelligent, much unlike what I had been feeling in the past year, but I declined, although I instinctively knew my liaison with Roger would soon end. I guess I understood how heterosexual marriages with children, mortgages, cats, dogs, and children can turn into nasty arrangements in which one person could lose money and the other, dignity. After all these years it almost made sense to me that *gringos* seemed to love their pets more than they loved their relatives or their neighbours. Finally, we went to Paris, which was to be the jewel of our trip. I was stunned by its beauty and it monumental power, but mine was a dry emotion. Fuck *Le Metro, le troissième arrondissement, Le Mairais,* the *Louvre,* the *Arc de Triomphe, la Tour Eiffel, y la puta que me parió* – I mean, who fucking cares if one is traveling someone else's trip! The whole thing felt like a rite of passage.

ROGER AND CAMILO GOT BACK TO VANCOUVER. While they were away, Roger's daughter had almost set the house on fire while she was high and had passed out in the bedroom. His son announced that his girlfriend was pregnant. Roger remained imperturbable through all of this news, made a couple of steely remarks as he wrote cheques to pay for the repairs and the abortion. Camilo found a message from Sol Ariega who said that she had gone to Montreal for the season to study and had left her son under Andrew's care, a startling thing to do in a country obsessed with child molestation and pedophilia. Garth wasn't completely happy with the arrangement, he liked absolute tidiness and control, but he did not dare to complain because he knew that Andrew was completely inflexible when it came to matters of loyalty.

Days after their return, Camilo was told that his application to graduate studies had been rejected. Outraged, he did some snooping and discovered that members of the applications committee had argued that he didn't have enough experience as a teacher in Canada and that the topic he had proposed, AIDS education, was not relevant. This came as terrible news. For days he tried to get Roger to intercede.

"C'mon, Roger, you're an insider, you can pull some strings," he pleaded in the sweetest tone he could muster while letting a stranger Roger had brought back from one of his shopping sprees fuck him in their bed.

"I can't interfere, that would be unethical," Roger responded demurely, catching his breath as he took the stranger from behind.

"Are you guys really into this?" complained the guest.

"Oh yeah, give it to me, harder, harder," Camilo gasped for air at the bottom of the human heap. "C'mon, Roger, surely you can do something."

"That's nepotism." Roger's decree was authoritative and categorical. The stranger lost his patience and pulled out, and the three of them lay side by side, their bodies smeared in sweat and Crisco.

Camilo insisted, "C'mon, Roger, I bet you can."

The stranger intervened, "Yeah, Roger, give the Latin bitch what she wants so she'll shut the fuck up! I'm losing my boner here, man!" and then he shoved his soiled cock down Camilo's throat.

A week later, Camilo's application file for graduate school was reviewed. It was discovered that a decision had been made without a complete file. No one uttered a single word of support or apology, but Camilo went ahead and presented an appeal that was accepted.

The day he turned twenty-eight, almost six years after he had come to Canada, Camilo sat by the curb on Pender Street and waited for Andrew to fetch him in his beat-up Volkswagen. He was moving out. He took the few things that belonged to him in a box: books, clothes, and photos, not much more than what he had when he had moved in. As he was leaving the house, its ghost, the cats, the golden credit cards, the sexual misdemeanors, the disaffected adolescents standing by the door, and Roger's tough-love smile – a portrait of Canadian gothic – Camilo cried bitterly. Andrew's car wriggled down the street and turned a sharp corner.

"Did he hit you?" Andrew asked.

Camilo shook his head. "Roger would never do that. He thinks he's too rational for that."

Andrew furrowed his brow. "I don't get it."

"Well, remember how I told you lots about Gabriel and our relationship, that sort of if-you-love-me-you-hit-me thing?" Andrew nodded in reply and kept his eyes on the road. "Well, I think this was the same, except that in this fucking *gringo* world – no offense – we even . . . what's the word – disembody, that is the word! We even disembody the way we inflict punishment." There was a long pause; the rain had started to beat hard on the roof of the clunky car. Camilo added, "Roger let others do the hitting for him and it just looked like play. Only once I got him to be himself and give it to me. Only once." They remained silent the rest of the ride to Andrew and Garth's place on Victoria Drive.

Camilo stayed with Andrew, Garth, and Sol's son while he looked for a place to live. Then out of the blue, Mariana Nomeolvides caught up with Camilo and told him she was going to Vancouver and, by way of explanation, she enigmatically pointed out that she needed a break from her highfalutin' life in Miami.

"I don't think I have a lover any longer," she sighed heavily.

"Do you have money?"

"Sure I do, *his* money."

"*Más vale diablo conocido que otro por conocer*, let's shack up together for a while."

"What about *your* husband, darling?"

"We're not together any more."

"Welcome to the club." They laughed acridly.

MARIANA WAS IN A PERMANENT STATE OF GLAM-
orous deterioration, much like Liz Taylor. Her relationship with the Chilean mafia guy had gone sour
and she had decided to save her ass and get out of
Miami. Goodbye Coral Gables and swimming
pool (and pool boy). She took some dirty money
and credit cards and flew to Vancouver. That
woman has a knack for ill-fated relationships.
Cesar and Andrew always commented that being a
fag hag had gravely altered her heterosexuality. She
expected straight men to be funny, interesting,
well-dressed, and courteous, but even queers were
not like that. Not only had she fallen for many fags in our coterie –
she had even once declared her hots for Italo – but also her dubious
boyfriend and silent partner with whom she had opened *El Goce
Pagano* those many years ago had turned out to be a repentant leftist
extremista with a penchant for young chicken – but I would only learn
about these six degrees of separation between Mariana and Ramiro
in London much later.

In any case, my immediate concern was to have a place to live so I
told Mariana that one should stick to one's kind and both of us being
Chilean – a white lie. Probably, Chela was the one who behaved most
generously towards Mariana; she said that it was a "girl thing" and that
she could relate. I felt that I would be okay living with her for a while,
so long as I frequently called Chela in Chile to get advice. They were
close friends too, although they never exchanged much correspon-
dence. Mariana had given Chela her first break at the underbelly of
Santiago's showbiz and Chela had always shown gratitude. When
Mariana decided to follow her lover to Europe – little did she know,
he was already chasing after boys in mini-skirts – Chela offered to
manage Mariana's nightclub so she could be free for a while to go and

try her fortune abroad. Mariana also dreamed the American dream so much.

When I reflect back on those times, I see that ours was some kind of exile, that's what it was, it wasn't as heroic as the partisan political flight, but a period of time in which we all seized in one way or another the few opportunities we found to leave a country that we never thought would break free from its insular mentality – it seems that it never did. One by one, we all found ways to get away. Mariana's globetrotting could leave one breathless; it was not easy to keep up – or to figure out what she was scheming each time. I remember hearing that Mariana and her lover had gone to Argentina on holidays, and after that I heard news through Chela that Mariana and her beaux had trekked to Germany – this was around the time I graduated from university and went on to teach for a year. Apparently, their accidental "honeymoon" in Europe had been exciting but momentary. Chela had told me that times got tough when Mariana's lover began to disappear for days and would come back home high on Ecstasy and reeking of sex. Entrepreneurial as she was, Mariana promptly exchanged her aspirations to a European lifestyle for a permanent tan, deep cleavage, noisy gold bracelets and rings, and a joint-venture with a seedy Cuban chap. Now, she was at a new crossroads in her life and the police were on to her Cuban man and whatever business they had going – much of it sounded like it happened out the back of a truck – and she had decided to come to Vancouver. She would still not discuss what her connection with this province of Canada was – and I did not ask again.

A few days after Mariana and I moved into a shabby apartment together on the edge of Strathcona Park, Roger called to tell me that I got a letter from the university confirming that my application to

graduate school had been reconsidered and accepted. I had many bitter words for Roger on the tip of my tongue, but I swallowed them.
Now, I had tuition fees to pay and little money. I had been sending
money to my mother every month and whatever I had left covered
the rent and bills. The work at the immigration department was
dwindling. So, I swallowed my pride and went to Roger's house to
collect the university letter, and took a loan from his altruistic albeit
heavy hand.

In July of that year, I became a Canadian citizen, a hyphenated
Canadian: not a true CBC (Canadian-born Canadian), but then no
longer an FOB (fresh off the boat). The joke didn't sit well in my stomach. I phoned my mom to tell her that her son was now a full-fledged
inhabitant of a different country, but I could have been talking about
Saturn, for all she knew. At the citizenship ceremony, the media and
political hotshots were in attendance to shake our little immigrant
hands. Photographs were taken, I posed with two red-suited hunks,
RCMP officers with thick moustaches and immutable, chalky smiles –
a cross between Santa Claus lookalikes and Chippendale dancers.
Their uniforms looked crisp like gift wrapping, I could peel it off
layer by layer with my teeth. I pledged alliance to my inner queen and
prayed to God to save the queer.

After I left the haunted house on Pender Street, I would often run
into Roger in the stores along Commercial Drive. He would introduce me to his boyfriend *du jour* and I'd feel the loneliness I had felt
before I went to Cuba, before I met Roger. If I ran into him at the
faculty club, he would address me politely and dismiss me in a few
public sentences. During those times, I wrote long letters to Leandro,
to my mother, to Ramiro, to Sol Ariega in Montreal. To Chela, I
wrote long and tangled litanies. Slowly, writing became a way of life.

If I had to thank Roger for anything, it would be for pushing me to sorely comprehend the eccentric *métier* of academic discipline that is at once captivating, isolating, and neurotic. As I practiced what is pompously called the scholastic disciplines, my body and soul morphed in ways I never imagined before. Some desolate nights I knocked at the scarred Trotskyite's door to wordlessly ask for a mercy-fuck. Once I went as far as asking him to be my lover, but he gently declined.

"I don't play consolation prize. Why don't you try and do some AIDS activism? It might make you less self-absorbed. Something good could come out of all those silly prevention workshops and volunteer training sessions. You will meet a guy."

"A guy?!" That convinced me. I gave it a real good try, but all I found in those tedious training workshops and support groups were happily coupled men with middle class intentions, or men who were too defeated by their illness to do anything other than wallow in it. I found guys who would otherwise have had no future. Other than that, the local AIDS organization was populated by overzealous and self-righteous earnest young activists who looked like skinheads but had the mindset of Victorian spinsters. White boys doing AIDS work, pristine examples of equality and compassion who wouldn't be caught dead with an infected guy, much less if he was an ethnic type, unless, of course, he was drop-dead gorgeous. It so happened that activism was a deadly serious affair too. I had to find a more challenging angle to that boring preaching-to-the-converted.

Chela wrote me a letter about how guys we knew had started to show signs of the epidemic. She told me that the health authorities were doing nothing; she was well informed and was looking to get a group of men together to do something about it. Aided by the Trotskyite, I began to secretly gather surplus ZIT, or was it ZAT? – it was some acronym I can't remember now – and there were other costly medicines given to infirm guys. There was so much controversy about the pills that some guys would pick them up from the pharmacy but wouldn't ingest them, ever. Instead, they would resort to fetid infusions, powdered fish cartilage, shriveled testicles of big mammals, or exotic fruits sold by charlatans. Others would just rub their amulets, crystals, and crosses; the new West Coast Buddhists would chant longingly for hours. I'd put my most subtle moves on them, knowing that Anglo men, in particular, scare easily like raccoons. I'd target the ruined West Hollywood types, men who only a few months ago had been rippled, robust beauty queens abandoned by their peers when the first give-away lesion had bloomed, when their energy had dwindled and they had to come back to Vancouver to enjoy the universal medical system they considered their birthright. It wasn't long before I had a few suppliers-cum-fuck-buddies. I spent long evenings by their side, stroking their ego as they reminisced about the sultry nights spent in the arms of red-haired Scandinavian admirers, dark Mediterranean lovers, high-strung French adorers, and potent German masters — *todas ellas, pero toditas ellas iban a ser reinas*. In more than one case I helped some of them exhale their last brittle breath, discreetly that is, helped by the cryptic directives from physicians who could never get their hands dirty because they were working for "a larger cause" — that's what they said. I'd hold them by their shaky hands to the light, always toward the light. With the reserved expression of a bartender stationed behind a counter, as displayed in postcards of those heavenly retreats that are decked with emerald green pools, I would carefully mix drugs following the instructions in a book called *The Last Exit* and place a little colourful umbrella against the salted rim of the glass — *na' niña, muerete tranquila, que lo comido y lo bailado no te lo quita nadie*, this I thought but never said it, these girls were too sad to be cheered in any way. I would then carefully package unused or unfinished bottles of pills and ship them to Chile. Chela became the AZT queen of Santiago, they called her *la Diosa química*, dispensing hope in little white and blue "dolls" with the cautious help of a local physician.

IN 1990, AFTER NEW YEAR'S EVE, CAMILO FLEW to New York. Cesar looked fatigued but contained when he picked him up at the airport. Their first stop before going to his apartment in The Bronx was at the hospital to visit Juan. Juan looked terrible. They talked to him in short phrases with feigned cheerfulness. Richard, his old lover, was there too, sweet and gentle, strong as a rock. Juan's mother was also there. Cesar had moved mountains to get money and a special immigration permit to fly her over from Chile. She had crossed the continent from summer weather to below zero temperatures to be with her son, to sleep in the uncomfortable hospital cot at the foot of his bed, and learn in a matter of hours the why, how, when, and where of Juan's illness and gayness. Half-convinced, she repeated to Camilo and Cesar what she had learned from Juan and the Spanish-speaking personnel at the hospital. She said that he would be fine, recover his weight, walk out of there, and see the sun again. Camilo spouted platitudes like beads in a rosary, one after the other. In the following weeks, Cesar and Camilo visited Juan in the late afternoons. They talked about Broadway shows, phone sex lines, Grace Jones' disco days, Madonna's questionable sincerity, and their past in Chile. His mother never, not once, shed a tear.

GETTING TOGETHER WITH ITALO WAS ANTI-climactic, but I thought he would distract me from the vision of Juan's suffering and his puzzling mood swings. Italo seemed unmoved by any of this and barely mentioned it in passing. Now I see how scared he must have been. I was terrified. He said that he didn't have much time to go and see Juan because he was working hard and dating a Jewish publicist who didn't know he was *Latino* – he had told him he was Italian – or that he was positive. What was all that about? I didn't give a shit, given the present circumstances. Sitting in a café near the Village, I realized that ghostly sights were everywhere. Someone told me later that day that Rollerina, the colourful drag queen on skates, had disappeared, and along with her, the fairy queen and many others. Italo and I didn't talk much about anything else. We ended up going to a bathhouse, our relationship demoted to a shallow camaraderie. Coincidentally, it had been Italo who first took me to a bathhouse in Santiago many years before, *Las Delicias*, a seedy place where upper class queens and working class fellows mingled in the well-commissioned privacy of the changing rooms. Beefy attendants showed us to the lockers, offered brutal massages, cold beer, and a no-frills fuck, but no kissing (too intimate), and no small talk (too busy keeping it up). The handsome and sly hustlers who roamed the joint would do it with us for nothing because we were young and cute. In this seedy bathhouse in New York we receded further into the dark, we did it through glory holes, not wanting to see the body on the other side, keeping human contact to a minimum. That night I wrote a long letter to Leandro where I imagined with no restraint that I was next to him, far away from all of this, under the sweltering sun, surrounded by so much life. Weeks later, I would receive news from him, he always responded with particular patience and sweetness, in short scribbled notes, telling me how much he wished he were with me.

OVERCOME BY SADNESS, CAMILO SAID HIS GOODBYES and returned to Vancouver, to its rainy winter nights. He told Andrew that all in all this monotonous town seemed friendlier than the enormous solitude of New York. He went back to school and part-time work. Compulsively, he began to read up on diets, complimentary therapies, and miraculous cures. He made it a habit to walk down to Circling Dawn on Commercial Drive to empty shooters of wheatgrass and spirulina, bottoms up. Later that spring he joined a gay dating service and listed his physical attributes, carefully enhanced but not fictitious, for strangers to peruse: 5'5", late twenties, brown, 8" uncut, Catholic, and educated. He got a couple of unsuccessful blind dates, guys who were horny but did not want to put out, guys who wanted to "take it one step at a time," guys who were pleasant but who were invariably tied up in another relationship, and guys who would run for the hills when Camilo told them he was positive (although he had seen them at the bathhouse a week earlier, their legs flailing in the air). One day he got another "match" by mail and phoned a man with a hoarse but sexy voice who lived in Seattle. They set up a date in Seattle for the following Friday. Camilo caught an afternoon Greyhound and met him at a downtown hotel at seven o'clock sharp. Their encounter went on systematically, without any sparks. Around ten, he mustered enough courage to tell him goodbye, and Camilo went on his way to the clubs on Capitol Hill.

WAS THAT DATE EVER A FLOP! I MEAN, HE TURNED out to be a fine black guy but with the conversation skills of a doorknob. It's not that I don't respect people's closets, but I've always found black closets particularly deep. I counted my losses, I had taken the time and money to get to Seattle – not to mention the added aggravation of being harassed at the border – so I headed for Club Z, a place I knew because in the two years I lived with Roger we had gone there several times on our way to San Francisco. It was a dark and large bathhouse, smothered in Crisco and reeking of poppers. It was a nocturnal zoo filled with raw moans and spikes, anxious animals sheathed in leather. Intense eyes lurking everywhere, pacing up and down, exuding glands, pulsating hearts; unleashed creatures in a jungle of harnesses, chains, straps, ripped jeans, and metal claws digging into flesh. After a benevolent hand fed me a serious joint, the huge bathhouse turned into the arcade of a cathedral, and I felt like a sacrificial lamb, willing and vibrant. *Este es el cordero de Dios que quita el pecado del mundo. Dichosos los invitados al banquete celestial.* Was it Madonna who sang that? Like a child I peeked into doorways and discovered imposing leather Buddhas sitting spread-eagled on wooden thrones, slitting the night with their shrieks and lamentations, chained by their necks and wrists. Time became immemorial. *Y así, medio soñando, medio rezando, me fuí por los corredores, cuando de pronto, detrás de una puerta semiabierta, se aparece el.* I let myself go in the hands of a stocky white man with a firm wide belly, *mezcla extraña de cancerbero y penúltimo polizón al exilio,* a harnessed chest like a big drawer with two silver handles, muscled biceps with a tattoo coiled around them, the small top part of the index finger missing, *el tango original, como el pecado, se baila entre dos machos al compás de un bandoneón piazzolissimo,* the close-up revealed a million details to me, a black ink barbed-wire tattoo around his left biceps, and down under, sticking out of a thick leather contraption, a solid member speared by silver rings through his frenum and around the head – it was like a penis resting on a futuristic wheelchair!

Sex with strangers is comforting and profound, but the let-down is brutal. When the chilly morning air filtered through the broken black glass in that bathhouse room and I came to my senses, I was exhausted and almost unable to move. Our sex was – I can't really find a word – ferocious? avid? What was most surprising was that, when we saw the morning light we didn't immediately turn away and leave – we talked! Philip was his name, and he said that he loved that I could swear like a trucker and be fucked like a lady. I smiled. Then, he offered that we see each other in the light of day.

The crude test of the morning light came. We survived it. Once we changed our costumes, Philip looked like an overgrown, grungy teenager. He was a gentle giant with a sharp wit and a twisted tongue, lots of patience, and an incendiary sexuality. We went for coffee at the Pike Place Market and then he asked me to come home with him – no strings attached. I accepted. What was not to like? We already had half of the deal clear, we knew we fit each other well sexually, precisely the reason why I had always preferred bathhouses to the stupid ritual of bars. I spent that Saturday evening locked behind doors, with my hands restrained behind my neck, subjected to his scrutiny and probation. Philip charted the lengths and widths of my body, appraising the crucial information contained in the torrents of bodily fluids and releasing it to baptize our newborn skin. When we finally arrived at a moment of lucidity, we realized that a cloudy night had been swept away by calm spring showers. We didn't eat, I remember crawling, panting, bumping against objects, ceasing to breathe, and then resurfacing again amidst scattered books and clothes, and I remember a white cat, Socrates, watching us judiciously from the windowsill. I told Philip it was impossible we'd made such a mess! He assured me that the place looked very normal. Sprawled in his hideous bed that looked like a torture rack with metal springs showing here and there, we looked at each other, awestruck, in exhausted wonder. Now what? We understood that this was a predestined meeting and we talked about it in simple terms, knowingly. That evening I managed to put myself together and he took me to the bus depot. At the gate, Philip asked me if I wanted to see him again. I'd already made a million plans to come back to Seattle. When I said yes, he kissed me long and hard right there in front of everyone.

IN THE DAYS THAT FOLLOWED THEIR ENCOUNTER, their phone lines suffered an international traffic jam. Mariana knocked at Camilo's door repeatedly to mumble that she needed to use the phone, but her roommate told her to wait, politely at first, derisively later. Camilo and Philip spent hours telling each other about their lives. Philip was forty-five, born and raised in Spokane, had two sisters and a brother, but he and his family only maintained a lukewarm relationship since his early coming out. He had entered the University of Washington, but he had been expelled after a year for reckless behaviour of some kind. After that, he got work as a cook, drank heavily, and fucked half the gay men on Capitol Hill through the 1970s. One day, now fifteen years ago, Philip stopped boozing and doing drugs cold turkey, after he had been fired for setting the restaurant kitchen on fire while going through a particularly nasty withdrawal. Months later, he had found a job as a handyman and landscaper for various buildings around town. He had very few close friends and had never had a lover, Philip said he did not know why, and that it did not bother him. That was his life, plain and simple; he did not talk much and this suited Camilo fine.

After the first weekend that Camilo went back to Seattle to see Philip again he thought that Philip looked less handsome but more attractive than in his wet dreams. His Dickies overalls and his lovely red truck made him the stereotype of the working man. Camilo recorded each one of his impressions in long dispatches to Chela and Cesar. He described Philip as silent, seemingly stern, but that this façade was underlined by a biting, deadpan wit. Philip's muscles were bulky, and so was his gut. Camilo stated how much he appreciated Philip's love for food and that he wasn't obsessed with washboard stomachs and plucked chests. In a few words, Philip described his views on sex and men – he said that sex is mostly in one's head and attraction is most-ly about "attitude." They had gone for dinner on Broadway and were having their first heart-to-heart, one of the few they ever had – Philip wasn't given to endless processing of the emotional minutiae of everyday life, as Camilo was.

"I've got something to tell you before we go any further with this." Philip looked stern and handsome.

"So do I," Camilo said, holding his breath. "You go first."

"I like you. We fit each other good," and he paused, "but you need to know I am HIV positive."

Camilo sighed. "What a relief," he said, "so am I." Then they talked about the many times that they had gone through this awful confession and how they had been rejected by men who would not touch them with a nine-inch pole, but could fuck in the dark as long as they didn't know. Camilo explained that it was strange and com-forting to find both relief and doom in sharing a lethal virus.

From then on, they took turns visiting each other every week. Philip worked "flex days" to have longer weekends. Once Camilo finished his graduate course load at the university, he set out to write a con-voluted tract about sex and illness, and began to spend entire weeks in Seattle. Idiosyncratic but easygoing Philip was truly fastidious about one thing, his dahlias. "I love things that can die in the winter and come back to life again in the spring," he said. He grew them, taking care of each seedling under hot lamps in the basement, label-ing them, and, once they had bloomed into capricious shapes and colours, he would take them to exhibition fairs all over Washington State. He also took care of two flower beds at Volunteer Park and would tend to them while Camilo spent long afternoons reading under the trees, and watching Philip's muscles strain. They could not wait to get home and devour each other; sometimes they did not wait and would sneak into the conservatory in the evenings to have sex amidst the humid tropical leaves. During these intimate retreats, Philip tenderly trained Camilo in the complicated use of sexual props – some of which Camilo found repulsive at first, but he soon learned that objects make no judgments, people who use them, or do not use them, do. During football season, Philip would join acquaintances to go and see the Huskies play. Camilo stayed behind, alleging that this was more *gringo* education than he needed. Camilo would take these opportunities to *feng shui* Philip's amazing apartment clutter. He came across an entire wardrobe from the 1970s crumpled inside damp boxes in the basement. He threw away stacks of old moldy magazines, junk mail, and unopened letters, washed stacks of dishes and pots, and mopped the floors. One day, he went too far and when Philip came back from work he saw sections of his apartment he did not know existed.

"This is humiliating," he mumbled.

"You're a pig, all bachelor *gringos* are, but you're adorable," Camilo replied. Unexpectedly, Philip started to sob and Camilo, startled, consoled him in a sweet tone: "It's not your fault, you say it yourself that you're white trash. It's genetic. You'll have the chance to humiliate me later. I'm your pig every other time."

"You like that." Philip smiled and gently forced him down on his knees.

Juan died in june without ever getting his green card and without ever being able to go back to Chile. At the time, Cesar, Andrew, Garth, Sol, and even Mariana were visiting Philip and Camilo in Seattle. They were getting ready to go to the gay pride parade on Broadway Avenue when the phone call came from New York. Andrew immediately drove Cesar to the airport. That weekend Philip and Camilo were shaken. They stayed at home unable to do anything, exchanging few words, hypnotized by the television and holding onto each other like orphan cubs. Later that night they had sex more intensely than ever.

THE FIRST TIME HIS HAND TRAVELED UP TO THE centre of my body I felt Philip had entered a cavernous refuge of viscous and pulsating walls. I became innocent as a child as he made his sinuous way into my soft membrane, throbbing with life. *Señor, concedeme participar dignamente de este misterio, pues cada vez que celebramos el memorial de este sacrificio se cumple la obra de nuestra redención.* It was mystifying to entrust my biological existence to him, and I was thoroughly transformed by the awesome experience. No matter how many times Philip helped me go through it over the years, it was never simple. It made me confront my visceral fears. I could claim a body that wasn't mine before then, one that wouldn't be only a bloody canvas of surgical instruments, an impersonal test dummy of car and furniture designers, the next client of masseurs and dieticians, the realm of psychologists and military training. I know it all sounds esoteric or religious. I guess it was. One night Philip pierced both of my hardened nipples with surgical needles and hung silver loops from them. Gradually, I learned to endure the meticulous torture of my organs with wet leather bands, and the blues I felt in my soul healed as they were replaced by the blues on my skin. Nothing can sum it up well. I sensed this would be the pain that I would submit myself to one day in the future. I confronted my superstitions, trepidations, and cravings. I became thoroughly aware of my nerve endings, the tissues, the skeletal crevices, and the afflictions that were in my body. We exorcised the macabre spell of the instruments of the hospital ward, the prison, and the church. Chained to a wooden cross, I rejoiced in this atonement, and rapaciously asked for more. Kneeling in a pool of sweat, tears, sperm, and urine, I recalled the men who had used me and were used by me, a cast of a thousand eyes. I threw out many of the remaining thoughts of Roger and the years of loneliness. In hesitant calligraphy, I jotted down some of my wicked penance to Chela. She did not respond.

A few weeks later on the phone, after Juan's mother had departed to Chile with his ashes, I firmly insisted for the first time that Cesar had to leave New York.

"Maybe it's time for you to go back to Chile," I suggested.

"And do what? We came here to find freedom . . . and love – whatever that is – not to find money, or comfort. I'm not about to give up my dream, thin as it may be. It would be like accepting that Juan and many others died in vain. No fucking way."

"At least get out of New York. You can stay here, at Philip's, while I'm away in Chile. That will give you time to find a job and a place to rent."

"You're going to Chile?"

That same day I told Philip that I had been given a grant to do fieldwork in Chile. He had a hard time accepting this, but he knew I needed to go back. We agreed that I wouldn't stay a day over six months and that he would come to visit after three months, for at least thirty days, to break our separation in two. With a lukewarm grimace, he accepted the portion of the plan in which Cesar would come to stay with him for a month before he went to Chile and then house-sit while he was away. He might have wanted to say no, but he dared not say a word.

IN PREPARATION FOR HIS AUSPICIOUS RETURN TO the motherland, Camilo completed his reinvention, the reinvention that had started shortly after he had met Philip. Camilo carefully constructed a stark new look, the brave-new-world clone, also inspired by his liaison with the Trotskyite and ACT UP: goatee, tight 501s, Doc Martens, thick leather belt, biker wallet on a chain, and a buzz cut. He left Canada one day in October, and Philip was there to see him off. Twenty-two hours later, aching and exhausted, he arrived in Santiago at the break of dawn. Uli, Chela's radiant twenty-something lover, picked him up at the airport and drove him and his plentiful luggage to the city in a small rickety car. Initially, Uli was polite but guarded, and he was visibly taken aback by Camilo's change in appearance and demeanor. It would take some weeks for the two men to warm up to each other. Camilo arrived on a Saturday morning, and Chela did not come to the airport because she was preparing "a new and improved show" that would premiere that night. They would see her then. Coming into the city from the airport, Camilo's eager eyes saw Santiago emerge slowly, suspended in its perennial haze of rarefied air, boxed between the Andean mountains and the coastal range. His ears were assaulted by the phenomenal noise, the droves of people hurrying along busy streets. Chela's house was an old and spacious adobe construction located in a dusty working class *barrio* called *Pudahuel*, far away from the maddening downtown. At the door they were greeted by Flavio, the servant, a thin, androgynous figure with patches of dark hair hanging loose here and there, curly nails like a lizard, a high-pitched voice and beauty queen mannerisms. At 5'3" and with a barely disguised middle-age complexion, Flavio lived his life to emulate Morgan Fairchild, making showy arrivals at *El Goce Pagano* on weekends – in fact, Flavio so ardently wanted to be a girl that he insisted on being called Flavia Morgana. Uli would have none of that and tersely addressed him as Flavio, but the rest of us called him Flavia. This exuberant creature gave herself completely to domestic life as a form of art: she did the laundry, ironing, cleaning, grocery shopping, and cooking – four meals a day if everyone was at home. The house was a jungle plagued by the shrieks of fleeting birds that seemed to clog Flavia's throat. The small butler-cum-maid took an instant liking to Camilo because he treated him nicely, in contrast to Uli's disdainful instructions. Upon his arrival, Camilo dropped heavily and fatigued onto an old couch wrapped in moth-ridden purple velvet. When he woke up later that afternoon Flavia, looking like an exotic bird in an opulent cage, floated ethereally from the kitchen to the living room to offer the contents of a platter, a heap of carefully displayed wedges of watermelon.

"*Pa'que se le remoje el paladar pues,*" Flavia smiled solicitously. "*Mire que esta noche es fiesta y debe estar como reina.*" It was the beginning of one of many Saturday night rituals.

Chela had left precise instructions for Uli to take Camilo to the infamous *El Goce Pagano*, which she now managed and where she was prominently featured on weekends. Uli gathered an entourage of *locas*, some of whom Camilo knew from before he had left Chile; they rejoiced in their meeting, cross-talking animatedly. They took turns examining Camilo from head to toe, marveling at his transformation, squealing at the sight of his piercings, and joining in gleeful repartee. Later that evening, past midnight, at the time hundreds of men make their sacred weekend pilgrimages to gay dance floors, the noisy group made its conspicuous entrance at *El Goce Pagano*. They promptly ordered combustible *Entre Sàbanas*: cognac, triple sec, sugar, a hint of grenadine, lemon and orange juice, a mix so powerful that it could numb the bombastic treble and bass of the dance music. Periodically, the DJ would slow the frantic beat down to a ballad and a rumour of sighs would ascend in the air as arms and torsos reached out to sway to the slow tempo. Camilo ran into a parade of acquaintances he had not seen in many years. *El Goce Pagano* remained unchanged, an over-crowded hangout, a remnant of the clandestine and bohemian years in Santiago, a scene that was about to change forever as American commercialism camouflaged as gay liberation made its inroads into Chilean culture. The lights were dimmed so low no one could tell what crawled up the walls or what was being poured into those slippery glasses. Camilo was told to keep track of his pockets as the place was still frequented by a miscellaneous audience: pick-pockets, flaming queens, tough guys, hustlers, pimps, menacing-looking dykes, and the odd incognito priest, a parade of bodies still untouched by the North American obsession for diets and protruding muscles. The patrons, whose silhouettes were shattered by violent strobe lights, looked like ghosts boogying in a fog of smoke and dry ice. The many dark corners of the venue crawled with lustful inhabitants, embracing, fondling, and kissing. Someone reassured Camilo that the police did not burst in with their German shepherds as often as they used to, with machine guns in hand, asking for IDs, pulling out the minors. In the old times, the owner of the joint, Mariana Nomeolvides, had to entertain the cops at the door, flirting long enough so her under-age clientele could get away by jumping out the small back bathroom windows or trying their luck in the rat-infested storage room.

Camilo stood there, mesmerized, recalling adventures and tawdry romance, like the time they were all taken to a nearby police station and held overnight, including Mariana, and by the break of dawn they had improvised a salacious drag show which had all the cops enthralled. Many a love story between the kids and the sturdy *carabiñeros* flared up that night. Camilo dated a young, dark cop, *un sureño* from the far south, whose bulletproof heart, or so he had told him, he had trespassed. But Camilo broke it three weeks later when he told the cop to go and blow his own horn. Camilo had been fooled by the

size of his gun and his uniform – wasn't everyone in those dictatorship times? – Camilo said, "*Mucho ruido y pocas nueces,*" a devastating
statement at best.

At three in the morning, the lights were extinguished and for five
long minutes the club was pitch dark, no exit or emergency lights. A
few hands groped the neighbouring bodies. A tenacious young man
with green eyes and aquiline nose who had followed Camilo as soon
as he walked into the place took this opportunity to be very forward,
moving dangerously close and whispering in Camilo's ear that he
liked him, that he could guess Camilo's bent, and that he could "see
to that." Camilo checked his wallet in his front pocket and responded decorously, in a wet whisper to his ear, that although he was permanently engaged, he would not mind his company for the night.
Such were the *sotto voce* provisions being made in the dark when all
of a sudden there was a screech, a blinding flash, and a glass ricocheted
against the floor. Chela, divine, emerged centre stage, blurred by the
dry ice clouds and accompanied by the loud cha-cha music. She was
radiant in a spectacular red-sequined dress and crowned by a million
white feathers. Four young studs, scantily clad, picked her up, twirled
her in the air, and put her back down without losing a single feather.
She was a cross between a female Elvis in pumps, an out-of-control
Liberace, and Walter Mercado, the well-known Puerto Rican
astrologer on Univision. After the frenetic opening number, she sang
a torch bolero with her own voice against a recorded soundtrack. Her
ten years of practice had surely paid off. She still had her *gringa* accent,
and made funny mistakes, but showed an unsurpassable command of
Chilean slang. Her quick comebacks were incisive and scary and the
audience heckled and laughed. Someone handed her a drink and a
silk scarf to dry her forehead. At that point she zeroed in on Camilo
who was standing close to the stage, by then firmly embraced by the
tenacious young man.

"Hello, you big *loca*, *bienvenida*." Chela toasted Camilo, drained the glass, and tossed it back into the audience.

After a breathtaking, acrobatic spectacle of contortionists, dancers, strippers, and other drag queens, mere runners-up, Chela gave a brief but frank announcement about safe sex and left the stage amidst the closing musical curtain. Later, she came to greet her friends, free of make-up, wearing a snug-fitting yellow sarong with big blue flowers, and gave Camilo a long and tight embrace. Tears welled up in their eyes.

"I see you don't waste your time!" she said to Camilo, or maybe to his young suitor, who then quickly disappeared into the crowd.

"Darling, the heart is private, the ass is public," responded Camilo.

Chela smiled. "You watch out, darling, that one is dangerous, a gypsy – *un gitano de verdad* – who carries a big knife in his panties. Don't you lose your purse this early in the game." Then she appraised Camilo, made him turn around, quickly ran her manicured fingers over his tight t-shirt to feel the nipple piercings. Confidentially, in Camilo's ear she affirmed: "I can see you have made 'the change' yourself, dear. You look good, like a man, I mean." They toasted "the change" and joined the party. Then they all left together at around seven in the morning and headed for one of those sordid downtown Santiago restaurants to catch the traditional hangover breakfast. Chela said hello to every night owl there: the night guards, the early morning shift workers, the late shift hookers, the insomniac diehards, the desperate queers in search of a last-call sexual fix; everybody. There, as they had *café con leche* and *pan de huevos*, Camilo and Chela caught up with each other's life, interrupted by repeated brawls at the front door between tousled wailing *locas* and horny thugs who wanted to beat them up. As Camilo and Chela carried on in English, the others in the entourage began to drift away, one by one, into the cold morning; Uli stayed, soberly drinking his coffee.

"Don't you go parading *el culo* at the Cerro Santa Lucia." When she realized she had switched to English, she added, "*¡Por lo menos ponle un condón antes de sentarte en el, rica, por lo que mas quieras!*" Chela warned the last of them as he embarrassedly zigzagged to the door. She turned to Camilo. "*Son como las perras, en serio, se calientan y ya está.* You know, I have kept all your letters," she said, quickly changing the topic.

"Me too," said Camilo.

"So, what do we do with them? There is a story there . . . hmm, though I'm not so sure about this new 'leather' thing of yours."

"It's not new," protested Camilo. "Philip has made me see it in a different light."

"Well, dear, *Chilenos* see it in no light at all. Their version of the leather thing is to beat the shit out of each other when they are quarrelling – *tenerte a ti pa' la patá y el combo* is our local version of your carefully-rehearsed ceremonies." Camilo listened sorely, but Chela was not one to be cut short when offering an opinion. "Remember that man who beat you up before I met you, what was his name?" She didn't wait for Camilo's answer. "Yeah, remember '*Quien te quiere, te aporrea'?* or so the saying goes. If they love you, they hit you, right?"

"I have changed much since that time," Camilo stated firmly by way of response. "Maybe you can't see how. You know about changes."

"Now, now, let's not talk about 'the change' now, not today anyway," Chela said, and pointed toward a new scuffle that had broken out by the restaurant door.

The large house in *Pudahuel* was always full of friends, relatives, and neighbours on weekends. There was always abundant conversation, wine, and food. The delicious ritual was to get up late, have lunch at around three, take a nap under the grapevines on the back patio, get up for some warm tea and sweets, and talk until late evening. Every

Tuesday various friends would show up to play Telefunken, a complicated and boisterous card game. The scene was exquisite, cluttered,
and noisy. Flavia served small canapés and drinks. When they had a
chance, Chela took Camilo to all the joints where they used to hang
out. Uli would sometimes come along, if he was not visiting his *abuela*
Rubelinda in *La Serena*, or did not have his nose buried in textbooks;
he was now studying to be a lawyer at a local university. He was
acquiring a great interest in human rights, and in the future, Uli
would be instrumental in the legal process against those who had
"disappeared," political prisoners like his own young mother. Camilo
could tell that Chela kept a tight, yet subtle, surveillance on the young
man.

"These queens are voracious, darling! And envious," she
explained. "They are always on the prowl. Got to keep an eye on
him."

"He's a catch," Camilo concurred.

Chela had become royalty on the dark side of Santiago and was
treated as such. In *El Goce Pagano*, she reigned supreme. She would
book the most bizarre entertainment, always with the ulterior motive
of saying something about sex and illness to those who would not
otherwise have heard a word about any of that. One weekend she
would engage the troupe of *El Circo de Estrellas*, a circus that toured
poor *barrios*, a lewd extravaganza of demented, semi-naked, polyester-
clad drag queens, kitsch clowns, crippled jugglers, and suicidal contortionists who paraded their pitiful sequined garments under a drafty
tent full of holes. Chela herself would don an apron and sell cotton
candy, caramelized popcorn, and greasy deep-fried *churros* sprinkled
with lots of confectionery sugar from behind the bar. She had turned
this lugubrious locale into a strangely hot commodity, people from all
over the city dressed in party costumes came to see the weekend carnival. Uptown queens arrived in packs to dance to cheap songs per-
formed by a local three-piece rock band, eat Chilean hot dogs reel-
ing with mayonnaise, mustard, ketchup, and chopped pickled onions,

and feast their eyes on the *barrio* boys (who were selectively admitted for free at the door). One of their thrills was to be formally asked to dance – *¿Señorita quiere bailar?* – a *de rigueur* petition to which the uptown *locas* would giggle and demurely decline. However, after the third *Entre Sábanas*, the adamant suitors would come back and the fancy *locas* would gladly engage in tight *boleros* or *cumbias sabrosonas*. Chela acted as matchmaker between the low-class, straight *rotos* and the *señoritas* who would often disappear into the sheltering darkness nearby in various states of inebriation and infatuation. It was not unusual to give up one's wallet, voluntarily or involuntarily, in amorous exchange for a fling with a local. Scenes of unrequited love would often take place in such mercurial surroundings, sordid fights between young men over a two-timing *señorita* or provoked by spiteful *novias* or *esposas* who had been left at home alone and burst onto the scene to bust their man *in flagrante delicto* and drag them home. Often, these scuffles were quelled by Chela's doormen, two robust dykes who carried concealed weapons.

CHELA WAS THE INDISPUTABLE QUEEN OF HER world and she had extended her Margaret Thatcher-like rule to a fledgling organization of activists, most of them ex-members of the communist party or ex-seminarians from one order or another. Now she was the leader of the chaotic Board of Directors that barely gave the place a semblance of sanity and governance. They had soberly christened it *La Corporación del SIDA*, but everybody called it *Casa Chela*, for obvious reasons. I had arranged to participate in whatever educational activities they had, and to write a journal about them. To do this I had brought a letter from one of my professors and from an AIDS organization in Vancouver. In fact, they had written it for me after much red tape, but without much interest. At *Casa Chela* no one had the time for these formalities; they welcomed me so immediately and so lovingly that I was taken by surprise. Like in those animated cartoons, a hook had suddenly pulled me into a crazy conga line and I was swaying my hips trying to follow the rhythm. I guess all those years in Vancouver had turned me into a guarded animal in many ways. I tried to describe in my letter to Philip in Seattle that what I found at *Casa Chela* was extraordinary. The everyday was saturated with tragedy, drama, anger, illness, poignant stories, gossip, and sarcasm. Young men who had been thrown out in the streets by their families when they had found out about their infections sought temporary refuge there. So did fragile beauties infected and beaten to a pulp by their "tricks," or a remorseful straight lover, *un tapado,* and tough *locas perras* right out of jail who needed a place to stay. They had amazing stories about botched petty crimes, people's contempt, *la gente decente,* their night sex trade shifts, and the bloody fights to keep their trade turf — *¡Esa cuadra es mia, mi linda! A mi no me la quita nadie or le corto el paño a la maraca se me ponga por delante. Con lo que me cuesta hacerme un corte y después lavarme el sapo en un baño de restaurant por ahi —* I remember hearing bitter complaints from a streetwalking *loca* that her "colleagues" had tried to snatch away a "john" the night before and they had to have it out on the corner. One of them would invariably end up in *La Posta Central* with a deep cut and torn panties.

There wasn't enough time to tell or hear all the stories. Often, I stayed late into the evening listening to the convoluted tongues that spiraled up in the cold air of the old house in *Calle Tocornal*. We would prepare tea and chain-smoke cheap Belmonts while I wrote notes for some of these stories for my research journal. They urged me to write in detail for posterity – *anote pues, joven, anote porfavorcito, que quede para la posteridad, mire que voy a tirar la chala luego* – I'll kick up my heels and die soon, they said. The young man with green eyes was also there, his attention locked on me, which was flattering but eerie – it was only his fear of being singled out by Chela's iron finger that made him keep a cautious distance. Each person who set foot under that roof was spontaneously endowed with a cleverly chosen effeminate name, a tradition among Chilean *locas* and in that society at large, a cruel yet infinitely clever form of social satire that would keep flooding egos and their supreme tragedies in check. The young gypsy boy was called *Yesenia* in honour of a current popular Venezuelan soap about a *gitana*. Obviously, he was mortified every time someone called him *Yesenia* aloud in front of me, but he bit his tongue. He had been kicked out of the place several times before for having started fist fights and he was well warned by Chela not to do it again. There was *La Mazorca* – the corn cob – her teeth uneven and yellow; then there was *La Cienpiés* – the caterpillar – who used crutches, *La Niña Símbolo* – the telethon girl – who wasn't the brightest bulb in the marquee; *La Penny Silina* – who had contracted every STD in the medical manuals and many, many others. They all had their names, their stories, a warm cup of tea, a cassette player to listen to Charles Aznavour, Adamo, Lucho Gatica, and Palmenia Pizarro, and a place to crash for a few hours at the *Casa Chela* in *Calle Tocornal*.

CHELA WALTZED AMONG THIS GARISH COURT OF young gay men, looking like Janis Joplin in feathered bleached hair and colourful veils, breaking the thick waves of cigarette smoke to introduce selected buddies, "sisters," and volunteers to Camilo. She worked hard for them and they adored her. She could stop fist fights with one look, catch thieves before they had even perpetrated their deeds, and could leave the place late at night to go to her nightclub and not be mugged, given her special connections to the local underworld. She could deal face-to-face with the local police and health authorities, reconcile estranged lovers and friends, bridge social classes, assign blame and praise, dispense justice, consolation, wisdom, and condoms. Camilo and Chela often got into heady conversations. One day, not long after Camilo started his work at *Casa Chela*, and after an agitated meeting, they got talking about the remarkable lives of the regulars at *Casa Chela*. They had started in Spanish, but as the conversation became more acerbic than usual, they switched to English without even thinking about it, and tempers flared. An odd role reversal took place: Camilo was critical of *Latinos* and gays, and Chela seemed more forgiving than before.

"Chilean *locas* are complicated, darling, they never say yes or no; no means yes," said Chela with a broad gesture that made her many golden bracelets jingle.

"C'mon! The same argument has been used as an excuse to rape women."

Camilo's edict made Chela pucker her lips as if she were sucking a lemon. "I see your leather man has not beaten that bookish pomposity out of you." Dismissively, she kept going. "Wanna hear a theory? Chilean men are the product of a matriarchy of manipulative women. Mothers, sisters, and *novias* mindfuck them with approvals and rejections – not to mention giving or not giving them any –

hence, they tamper with the emotions of sons and husbands. Then, they complain about getting smacked! That is why us *locas* have to be like women with our men and like men to our women – get it? We're sandwiched in the middle. Don't you like getting sandwiched? What's not to like?"

There was an odd strength in the circularity of Chela's argument; Camilo recognized it but decided to oppose it. "Anyway, Canada seems so different. There is so much more respect for people. Gays don't have to be *locas*, behave so effeminately, they don't have to play those games."

"Honey, Canada is simply boring – been there, done that – anything so respectful and straight lacks passion." Then she resumed her train of thought. "The same thing happens with social class. It is extreme in Chile, true, but *gringos* conceal it under a veneer of equality. I *love* that! 'A veneer of equality,' you should write *that* down!"

"Doesn't all the bullshit about sexuality and class drive you nuts, though? It makes *locas* a bunch of pathological liars, always ashamed of poverty and sex."

"Aghh! You got mighty self-righteous after a few years up north. Admit it, there is value in all that social dance – you know it, you did it – *ojos que no ven, corazón que no siente*, it makes everything more bearable, *decente* as we say here."

"But, that 'don't ask, don't tell' policy is a big closet!" complained Camilo. "At least in North America gays and lesbians are legally protected."

"Bullshit!" Chela was now up in arms. "All that bogus gay liberation, *that* is a big closet. What have we got? That they are now legally enforcing that our 'lifestyle' is okay? But deep inside, it still turns their stomachs, if you're not young, gorgeous, witty, and with great taste." Camilo tried to get a word in but Chela sped up. "What you call the Chilean closet is more Catholic ambivalence than fear of who they really are. Yes, it's a pain in the ass, but it's far more palatable than the regulated freedom you're trying to defend – I know you, you're playing devil's advocate. Well, let's play, girl – I prefer a world plagued by *virgenes* and *puta*s than a world of clones who say they're 'bisexual' or 'versatile' while they're craving to get fucked and fucked raw; at least our *locas* are getting infected for love, not simply because they are too dumb to admit they are fickle and they like it raw. I prefer *this* world to a world where they say they don't care about social class or whether you're infected or not, a world where everyone is ever so conveniently 'out' or 'outed.'"

Camilo stuttered, "But – but – it's all so full of double standards, double entendres, double everything. Why can't they be more straight about stuff?" His unfortunate choice of words did nothing but incense Chela.

"Straight? What the fuck! You're defending the indefensible, that one world is better than the other. No, not with me, darling. You can say that *Latinos* are passionate and fickle. I'll give you that, but *gringos* are only the flip side of the same coin. They play the ice queen; we invented 'one-night stands,' 'recreational sex,' 'mercy-fucks,' 'sloppy seconds,' and 'fuck buddies' – we have a phrase for everything – but once we are hooked we are just as gullible as the next one. There, here, it's all a grand world of illusion, darling, don't you forget it – *la vida es espectáculo* – like La Lupe used to sing, remember? – *Puro Teatro* – *gringos* need to appear to be in control, it's the Protestant way, hard work, hard play, no hesitations, no ambivalence allowed, you're either queer or straight. The so-called 'gay liberation movement' shackles mystery and charm. So, don't come telling me that what you got there is better or worse, I won't accept that." By the end of Chela's tirade, the small group around them had dispersed, sensing that what had started as an animated chat in English had turned into something far more intense. Camilo's eyes had welled up with tears of humiliation. They had sat facing each other for a good hour after closing time.

Chela had softened her tone. "Don't cry. I see what you mean, but you're wrong if you want to forget what you are inside. I think that Roger fucked you up real good, baby, give it a rest. Don't you ever forget where you come from – I don't – and make the best of where you are now." When someone rang the doorbell, Chela slowly stood up and left the room. Camilo lit another Belmont and cried softly. Someone had just come in from the street, crying.

THAT CONVERSATION WITH CHELA MADE ME COME undone. She had taught me a lesson and somehow I agreed with her. That night Chela stayed behind to assist the lost soul who had rang the doorbell, and though it was fairly late I decided to walk a few blocks before catching a cab to the house in *Pudahuel*. Lost in my reveries, I had walked two or three blocks, mentally writing a letter to Leandro, when I ran into a trio of young men hanging out on a dark corner. I was alerted by their stare and the intense smell of weed, and made a rapid detour to cross the street, but one of the men moved quickly to cut me off. My heart missed a beat. It was the beautiful *gitano* with the slanted green eyes, the one chasing after me in *El Goce Pagano* and in *Casa Chela*, the one Chela had warned me about. I sighed in relief, and then the little wheels of my mind – always in synch with my genitals, and in general with my lower body – began to turn. I can't say what made me do it, maybe it was the dark night, the full moon, the softness of his touch that comforted me, the harsh words pronounced by Chela that had worked a spell on me. I don't know. *El gitano* and I spent the night together in a cheap motel.

A MONTH LATER, CAMILO AND THE *GITANO* WERE still meeting near *Casa Chela* and ending up at the cheap motel. Theirs was a clandestine relationship, and both seemed comfortable with the arrangement. In tentative words, the gypsy told Camilo that he had "a thing" with the guy who had bailed him out of jail. Camilo languidly replied that he did not care, and that he would not be interested anyway because he was in love with a *gringo* who would soon come to visit him in Chile. He also flatly told the *gitano* that he appreciated his energy and acrobatics, but that there was nothing to prove. Camilo's disdain did nothing but ignite the other man's desire and redouble his efforts; every time they met, the *gitano* tried unusual things to delight his part-time lover. Later, Camilo would play with him, when they were at *Casa Chela* or if they bumped into each other at *El Goce Pagano*, purposely ignoring him as if he did not exist, but brushing up against him if he had to go by, only to smell the sting of the young man's appetite. Camilo was learning how to flirt again and the *gitano* was his guinea pig.

One evening during a puppet theatre presentation in the common room at *Casa Chela*, the gypsy followed Camilo into the house's only bathroom and closed the door swiftly behind him.

"I'm in love with you," the gypsy blurted out. "I can be very good to you . . . don't make me jealous."

"Are you for real?" Camilo laughed as he tried to use the toilet. Outside the door a herd of screeching *locas* kept knocking and complaining – "*Ya pues salgan luego, que estoy que me hago pichi.*"

"I love you, even if you belong to a fucking *gringo*, even if you leave." His eyes were close to Camilo's as he tightly embraced him.

"It can't be. My boyfriend will be here soon. Why start something anyway?"

"Can't we just *see* each other?"

"Bullshit. We're too horny to do that, but we're now too close for comfort, aren't we?" The queue of *locas* waiting outside were getting really annoyed – "*Ya pues, dejense de hueas y salgan, que esto no es casa de putas.*"

"So you admit there is something going on?" The gypsy did not want to let go. "Are you embarrassed because you're infected?"

Camilo was startled by his knowledge of that information. "Give me a break!" Camilo said, pushing him aside. "How did you know that?"

"Gossip travels like wildfire. Everybody knows that Chela is infected too, and that her friends all have *sida*, they are all *sidosos*, but don't you worry about a thing, they all like you very much here, they would never tell anyone."

Camilo was taken aback by the news about Chela that the gypsy had inadvertently delivered, but he kept his poise. "Fuck, that's precious – they wouldn't tell anyone – obviously, everybody knows it, like they all know about *your* business, boy." Camilo pushed past the gypsy to leave, but after some thought, he paused for a moment and turned around. "I'm not concerned about them knowing anything about me, or about you and me fucking, there are plenty of condoms out there. I'm not concerned about your hustling either." Camilo's tone was cynical. "Isn't it amazing how we all feed the gossip and at the same time nothing leaks out of here?" After giving the gypsy a fleeting kiss on his full lips, Camilo savoured each of his last words: "You can get addicted to this, to how good it feels to get it inside – no latex," and after this *non sequitur* Camilo rushed out before the waiting line outside. "*Ay, por Dios, come se demoraron. ¿Y que estaban haciendo?*" they inquired enviously, but Camilo ignored them and returned to the common room where the safe sex puppet show was about to resume.

THAT WASN'T THE END OF THE *GITANO*; FOR SOME reason I didn't feel like ending it. In fact, thanks to the crafty services of Flavia, acting as a time-honoured *alcahueta* who panders to cupids and other lower-echelon angels, the *gitano* began to sneak into Chela's home to spend ardent nights with me. *Flavia's* favours were paid with my silence – I knew she often entertained in her quarters and that house was spacious enough for all of us not to meddle in each other's business. Having the *gitano* around waiting for me, yearning for me, flustered by my indifference, finding new ways of keeping me awake at night for hours, kept me interested. It wasn't so much the sex itself – our sex was a basic dogs-in-the-yard trifle – but the stuff around it was seductive: his short-fused, wiry personality, the extravagant lines he whispered to the back of my neck, the intensity of his green eyes when he refused to let me go in the mornings without taking me once more, and the way he could disguise the mechanics of safe sex as a shrewd diversion – he was surely good at his trade. Not to mention that it was flattering to have at my beck and call what others had to pay for. One could say I was catching up for all the years in Chile that I had missed, maybe I was having second thoughts about my borrowed life abroad. I was frank with the *gitano*, and it was at that point that we took a strange curve onto a different road. As for the news that Chela was infected, I kept it to myself, I didn't know what to make of it and thought I'd wait for the right occasion to broach the subject with her. As the time that Philip was to arrive quickly approached, I became more anxious about my amorous antics with the *gitano*. I tried several times to reason with him, that we needed to stop this. He agreed to stop while Philip was visiting. I said that we should stop for good and he responded that when a *gitano* lays eyes on someone, and casts a *conjuro* as he had done on me, it was a spell that would eventually make me decide to stay in Chile, with him, where I belonged. I reminded him of how bitterly he complained about his own people turning their backs on him and about *chilenos'* deep disdain for *gitanos*, and he responded with something about the matters of the heart that run deeper than the land.

Every minute that Philip was with me in Chile was a dream come true, far better than I had ever anticipated. I felt complete. We traveled up and down the long and skinny strip of land that is Chile, first to the south and then to the north. Everywhere we went, we were in each other's arms; we felt on top of the world, like those "A" list fags in glossy gay magazines. Our status as foreigners, the way we dressed, and our intimate use of English allowed us to travel in a sort of cocoon. I was seeing my motherland for the first time and I was seeing it through two pairs of eyes, all the gestures, the flavours, the places, seemed intriguing and delightful.

In Santiago Philip met my mother with whom I had initially felt distant. After over thirty years of work as a maid, she had recently retired. Together, the two of us had purchased a small house in a working class *barrio* where she had settled. I had decided to stay at Chela's because of the gay thing, being what it was, it was better managed by not flaunting it under the same roof. However, I had used some of my time judiciously to recapture and understand our mother and son relationship in a different light. I had changed so much and she was so much the same. The spell of the overbearing, manipulative mother expounded by Chela had been broken and we had to find new ways of relating to each other. Ours was a bittersweet victory over our destiny; my breaking away from Chile, and her victory – which would always be her pain – was to live her dreams through me, through whom I had become. It wasn't easy, but her usual unsentimental ways and lack of judgment helped. She immediately warmed to Philip and insisted on engaging him in long chats, even though he understood none of it. I guess it was one of those "you had to be there" situations, but Philip was never one for long-winded conversation – in fact, for any conversation at all – so my mother's fully spontaneous monologues left him dazed. Of course, we spent a lot of time with Chela, even with Uli – whom I thought was taken by Philip's odd and tough looks – and with the others at home and at the *Casa Chela*. Philip and Chela never really hit it off, I could tell, but they were congenial to each other. Philip never said much to her and she never tried to pontificate with him. Our best times were the long days that we reserved to be on our own. We walked the city in all directions, and in each street, each place, I had a story for Philip. He'd piece my former life together and say that it all made sense. In the evenings, we would go for quiet walks. If we were in Santiago, we would always be invited to visit someone or participate in some activity at *Casa Chela*. Later, at around ten, the time that Chileans often have dinner, we'd have a sumptuous supper somewhere. Our time together went by so quickly. The evening before Philip was leaving, he and I spent hours locked in each other's embrace. Philip spoke little, as usual, but he said a few things that made it clear to me how much I loved him and how temporary my sojourn in Chile was.

"I was a dumb *gringo*," Philip pondered seriously. "Now I get it when you say that *gringos* don't see past CNN. I'm so fortunate to have seen this other world because of you."

I said, "It ain't like in the movies, eh? Some stuff in this country, in this city, drives me crazy, but all in all it's a good place." When I heard the nostalgia in what I was saying, panic swept over me for an instant. I felt guilty for my affair with the *gitano*, for not having missed Philip as much as I should – this incredibly wonderful man – for having left him behind all those months to pursue a career, a future that probably meant shit anyway. I felt stupid and cried. Sobbing, I told Philip about the *gitano* – not out of Catholic guilt, it was loyalty – and he only smiled and lifted my chin, and kissed me.

"You yourself have said it before, that one cannot cage one's lover's cock or emotions behind a barbed wire fence," he reassured me.

"Oh, I was only bluffing – you know, I needed to look cool."

"You are cool."

So I collected myself and behaved 'cool.' I told Philip something like, "Now, come on over and take what is rightfully yours," while I got undressed.

That evening, the substance of our dedication to each other bled through every pore in our bodies. Sweetly at first, then we made ardent love, scratching, biting, yelling, then caressing, pressing, lapping every inch, we loved until we couldn't breathe anymore. It was March, the beginning of the Chilean autumn. How could I forget that evening, it probably foreshadowed the beginning of our autumn as well, but that evening we were so present in mind and spirit that it seemed that no contagion could ever come between us. As per our tacit agreement, we did not let any barriers separate our skins. The evening darkness cooled us and diffused the lines of our bodies into shadows. When the remaining blithe spirits plunged into the soothing pool of the night, we fell asleep embraced by a calming breeze.

ONE LOVELY AFTERNOON IN MARCH TWO WEEKS after Philip had left Santiago, Camilo sat with Chela on the back patio, a porch surrounded by generous flowers in bloom and shade, sipping warm tea served by Flavia. Camilo came clean with Chela about what had gone on with the gypsy, the doubts he had entertained, and what had transpired between Philip and him, and about Philip's amazing love. Chela offered her wisdom.

"*Linda*, you know how it is, it's happened to me. I mean, I came here to see whether this was my place or not – we all need to come back to decide whether to stay or leave for good. It's a strange kind of betrayal, but it's not about deciding whether one is Chilean or not, it's about places in the heart."

Camilo was pensive. "Funny you should say that, Chela, the *gitano* said something along those lines last time I saw him."

"Beware of that boy, darling, he's trouble, and now he is roadkill on your highway of love. He's lovely, but he's a hustler and a liar, don't you ever forget that."

Camilo seemed to recollect something very important, took a quick sip of his tea, then asked, "By the way, one day the *gitano* said something about you that I've been wanting to check with you. . . ." He paused. "I mean *Casa Chela* is always full of stories, it's hard to know what's true and what's not, that's why I needed to ask you. . . ." He paused again. Precisely at that moment, they heard someone knock at the front door, followed by a little yelp and the quick clacking of Flavia's flip-flops rushing to see who it was. A minute later, a handsome man showed up at the back door – behind him, Flavia made all kinds of prim gestures to apologize for the interruption. She had probably been eavesdropping and wanted to know what the end of Chela and Camilo's conversation would be. For a split second, they were all motionless.

"Hi Gabriel, come in," Chela said. She invited the man standing at the back door to step out onto the patio. "Camilo, this is Gabriel. He's dating one of my dancing boys at the club." Chela did a double-take – not one used to being caught by surprise – then quickly regained her poise. "Er . . . maybe you two have met before." Camilo stood up and they tentatively shook hands in silence while sizing each other up. The strong grip of the hand that had been raised against him so many times before made him shiver. Gabriel looked older, still very handsome, but a bit heavier around the waist, prematurely grey hair at his temples, and tiny wrinkles at the corners of his eyes.

"¿Quieren un tecito? ¿O Nescafé? Tengo aguita helada también, si quieren." Flavia could smell a tense moment when she saw one and had begun a rundown of the beverage menu when Chela's icy look stopped her dead in her tracks.

"Please sit down, Gabriel, have some tea. You look a bit frazzled, dear." The ensuing conversation was rather telegraphic and five minutes later Chela, who prided herself on being very quick on the uptake, simply announced that she needed to do some urgent grocery shopping, and that she and Flavia would not come back for at least an hour.

Befuddled, Gabriel stood up to kiss Chela goodbye on the cheek, as is the custom in Chile, and briefly snapped out of his present state to warn Chela. "Be careful, that nasty gitano, the one who always picks fights at the club, is standing at the corner. Who knows what he's up to." Camilo gasped and Flavia let out another little yelp.

Chela stood up to leave. "Don't worry, dear, we girls know how to take care of ourselves." Chela's eloquent glance in Camilo's direction was met with a confused expression. "Anyway, thanks for the heads-up, Gabriel. It is one of those days when everything seems to come around. See you later, Camilo!" She exited with her nose in the air and Flavia in tow.

Left alone with Gabriel, there was a long pause, as the afternoon seemed to huff a warm breeze over them. They said a couple of perfunctory things, but soon eased into conversation, studying each other with curiosity, not with that combustible mix of scorn and lust that had flared up so many times in the past. Drawing the lawn chairs closer together, they talked about the years that had passed and their composure was new to each other, enticing. Their conversation was oddly endearing but general, they didn't seem to be able to get into it as they saw they had taken such different paths in life; after half an hour, they sat in silence again. Then Camilo stood up and so did Gabriel.

"This is a chance to close an old chapter, isn't it?" Camilo smiled, his hand gently touching Gabriel's cheek. "Chela and Flavia . . . Flavio, won't be back for a couple of hours. That was awkward for a moment there, but I had never told Chela your name, or if I did, she didn't remember – our thing happened before I met her."

"She is a fine lady. She always hires me to do handy work around here." Gabriel ran his hand through his hair, drops of sweat appeared on his forehead, but he did not move away from Camilo. "I came today to check the kitchen sink. I brought my toolbox. I've got to repair the. . . ." Camilo kissed him steadily and tenderly. Gabriel responded in kind, then said, "She's a fine lady. They say bad things about Chela behind her back, you know – I hate it, they say she used to be a. . . ." The doorbell chimed, Camilo refused to answer it, knowing full well who stood out in the street.

"Shouldn't you see who is at the door?" asked Gabriel nervously.

"Never mind the door, it's probably a street vendor, they'll come back later," Camilo said seductively. They kissed again, this time with more intensity.

Gabriel gently pushed Camilo away. "No, you know we can't be doing this," he whispered.

"It's about your boyfriend, right?" asked Camilo. "This is the house of secrets, no one will ever know."

"No, it's about *you*." Gabriel's tone changed slightly.

"C'mon, Gabriel, this isn't the time for pointing fingers or – "

"It's not about that." Gabriel's tone was now weirdly sympathetic. "It's about your illness, I don't want to catch it. You're still good-looking and all, I'm flattered but. . . ."

Camilo froze, his face turning into a grimace. "Catch it? Who told you?" Before Gabriel could answer, Camilo held the palm of his hand up to halt any possible answer. "Never mind. Who said that you can *catch* it just like that?" He snapped his fingers.

"C'mon, you're trying to – I don't know what you're up to, I don't care, you should respect others – you're infectious." The sound of Camilo's open-handed blow to Gabriel's face was a whip cracking the dense afternoon air.

"Get the fuck out of here. Now!" Camilo commanded firmly. Gabriel smiled, clenched one fist, and with the other hand touched the reddened right side of his face, then slowly turned around and walked into the house. Camilo followed him inside to the kitchen where Gabriel picked up his toolbox, and then to the front door.

Heading to the gate, Gabriel turned around one last time. "May God help your soul."

"Fuck you," muttered Camilo.

"I knew you would always end like this." Having said this with infinite pity, Gabriel walked down the street. Camilo stood for a long time, unable to move, in pain and bewilderment, the afternoon sun hitting him right in the eyes, dazzling him. At last, he noticed that the gypsy was standing there, watching him.

"I told you to go to hell," Camilo said.

"Then, let's go together. *Los dos solitos.* I know Chela and that crazy bitch maid of yours are out." The gypsy pulled Camilo inside, playful, tickling him, kissing him on the neck, struggling with his clothes, jumping out of his light shirt and pants, no underwear, dropping his sharp pocketknife on top of the small pile of clothes. As they got naked Camilo began picking the items up, gathering the clothes, trying to steer the gypsy into his bedroom, afraid of being caught naked in the hallway.

A COUPLE OF MONTHS AFTER PHILIP HAD GONE back to Seattle, I realized that I didn't want to be away from him or stay any longer in Santiago. I wrote a long letter to Leandro in which, for the first time, I told him about Philip – there was lots to tell – and about the doubts I had while I was in Chile and how I have decided it was time to leave. My work at the *Casa Chela* was almost done. I also felt an uncanny sense of risk. I didn't want to let new roots grow that would fasten me to that soil again: the Chile I had left over ten years ago, in a state of siege, under heavy military repression, underdeveloped and malnourished; the Chile in which I had convinced myself I'd have had little chance to fulfill my ambitions, but I would never know for sure what could have happened; the Chile I loved intensely but where now I could only fit as a visitor. The Chile that was disappearing before my eyes, carrying away my dear ghosts and my childhood dreams, washing away the traces of many of its inhabitants, people like Uli's disappeared mother, who didn't even have a ghost – Chile was an old and tired country that had left behind deep scars and resentment. Everything was being replaced with modernity, covered up with manicured lawns, high-rises, and unlimited credit to buy appliances. In this landscape of overblown success, our plague would always be a mere inconvenience and the *Casa Chela* an exotic limbo for the downtrodden. I was grateful that I had been given the opportunity to do the work, this I told everyone during my last meeting with them. We were gathered around a portable heater because the city was already turning cold. Sincerely, I had to admit to everyone and to myself that being able to leave was a measure of relief. I wasn't about to give up my life in Canada, no matter how unfamiliar and rigid it sometimes felt. From that moment on, I understood that no matter where I lived, I would forever be a foreigner inside my own skin. At the end of that letter to Leandro I promised him I would go back one day, once again. I didn't mention the gypsy at all.

The morning before I left Chile, someone phoned from an emergency room to tell me that the gypsy was there and wanted to see me. Instead of giving the phone number of a next of kin, he insisted that the nurse call me. She explained that he had tried to commit suicide with his pocketknife. I mumbled some confused excuse and said to tell him that I was leaving, that I would write. The nurse abruptly interrupted me to tell me that they had done a "test" on this "client" before — she punctuated each word as if she was talking to an idiot — and that the "test" had come back positive.

"Why are you telling me this?"

"We know our client is high risk due to his trade. We thought you should know, being one of his — one of his 'protectors' and all."

Camilo's voice quavered with anger. "Are you crazy? How dare you reveal this information to a stranger on the phone!"

"Sir, do not speak to me in that tone, please, or I will have to terminate this conversation. I am following procedure. I needed to inform you. You must come in for a test yourself." The nurse's tone was unnaturally officious. I hung up.

I couldn't face one more romantic and tragic cliché. I stayed awake for hours, wallowing in Catholic guilt. I had allowed myself to do this to him — hell! He had practically connived me into doing it! I reviewed the events of that night, a few weeks before. When I had told him that my return ticket was ready, he got into a crazy head space and insisted that he wanted me to give him something to carry with him forever — those were his exact words. He lit up the motel room, our habitual hideaway, with aromatic candles — how corny is that! — and put that damned Javier Solis bolero on instant replay — *pero esta vez/quiero entregarme a ti de una forma total/no con un beso nada mas /ya sea por bien o sea por* mal — all those lines about giving oneself up in body and soul to the only one you've ever loved. They conjured up an inescapable spell. I tried to give him a warning, but he muted me with his snaking tongue. What would a safe sex lecture have accomplished? I had done enough safe sex workshops to last me a lifetime. I simply refused him, but he played me for hours, played with my mind, pleading, he whispered, cajoled, and finally he had me inside, riding crazy, savouring the acidic flavour of a cliffhanger in my mouth, fueling my cock inside of him, shooting a million stars into him when the morning was about to break and hearing him cry and thank me softly a dozen times.

At the airport, the morning air was crisp and the sight of Chela in a knockoff Gucci ensemble, holding sweet Uli by the arm and waving goodbye with her jeweled hand, and the sight of Flavia crying profusely, all remains vivid in my mind. I told them I would always love them. After I left Chile, I'd never see the *gitano* again, but Chela kept me posted about his queer evolution. He had mellowed out; he had started to come more often to *Casa Chela*, to get involved as a volunteer in outreach and workshop activities, and later, as the organization grew, he started to lead some of the activities. Chela speculated that he had even stopped turning tricks for a living. Many years later, the *gitano* would be traveling around the globe as a career activist. We would all be queens, indeed we would.

My nausea settles in at dawn and stays all day long, a kind of drunkenness. My diarrhea is obscene. The ugly Trotskyite, my activist friend and bootlegging accomplice, died one Tuesday afternoon. It was weird to run into him at the hospital. Both of us looked like war casualties, and our suffering didn't allow us to have any camaraderie.

Helplessly we had tried to sneak into a washroom to be with each other, but one of the nurses condescendingly ordered us out, patted us on the buttocks like children, and told us to return to our rooms.

Leandro algunas veces tu recuerdo me corre por las arterias como un líquido caliente. Invoco tu nombre en la cúspide álgida del dolor, en Español, y las enfermeras no entienden, they say they feel left out — anybody who speaks a different language is seen as the one with the impediment and they see themselves as victims, I don't get it *y yo les digo que nada, que solo estaba gozando en mi lengua extraña. Si dejo mi imaginación volar afiebrada terminaré en La Habana como un insecto pulsando al sol, cruzado por una aguja hipodérmica, batiendo las alas que rasgan la mañana como un cuchillo gitano.* Yeah, yeah, just stick it in! No, it doesn't hurt one bit — done thicker needles than that — no, I'm not being rude. Okay, okay, I didn't notice I was speaking in English. I'm dictating a letter, can't you see I'm busy here? *¿Como se supera el dolor? Es fé y fascinación, es depojarse de la desconfianza, de los miedos y entregarse a un Dios desconocido como virgen de otra iglesia.* Who writes as I speak?

Two years! Philip and I were together for two years and some of that time I was away in Chile — how selfish is my God, that he only gave me two years of something that held so much promise and so much joy. One day Philip and I had an aching talk in which we swung open the doors to our fears. His health was evidently suffering by then. After coming back from Chile he was taking more days off from work, he was plagued by gastric infections. And I know — Cesar told me — the times that I had to be back in Vancouver to attend to school matters or to the bits and pieces of life I had there Philip would often stay at home and tend his dahlias in silence.

"What will I do if you're not with me one day?" I asked. It took guts to ask that question. "How would I live?"

Philip's oceanic blue eyes were calm and reassuring. "You'll hold onto three things," he said in a whisper. "My love, your friends, and your books, the things you love the most." We were quiet for a long time after that. Those words never left me. It's hard to explain how one begins to accept the drudgery of the everyday, even though every hour feels like a sharp, gelid blade cutting flesh or cutting flowers, one can hear it, like one hears every little trickle and step in the movies when they have rigged the entire set with mikes – one can even hear the heartbeat of the actors. Every other week, when we would return from another discouraging medical test, Philip would try another medication, have another couple of sick days, and then dig into his cluttered drawers looking for a smaller sized t-shirt or pair of pants, not saying a word. That winter I attended a conference in Montreal and stayed at Sol Ariega's, who was wrapping up her term there and getting ready to go back to Vancouver. As always, Sol was sensible and supporting, a great comfort for the soul. I was uninterestedly learning the Byzantine academic ropes, learning to speak in tongues to fend off any questions, to put others down with pedantic quotes; I was learning to wryly perform at conferences and speaking engagements – the middle class excuse for sexual tourism and relentless professional self-promotion. Like a good soldier, I'd go, see and – instead of killing – fuck the locals. The gay men I met at those events, particularly those booted skinhead activists, attracted me and at the same time repelled me. They could sit for hours and talk about cocks and asses, about fluids and sexual manoeuvres, about the tedious "identity politics," "solidarity," and "community," but they would recoil prudishly at the end of the evening when I told them to get laid, with me. Then, I'd rush to get to Seattle and be with Philip, wearing my heart on my sleeve, always wondering what new small detail would have changed in his appearance, fearing the worst, not knowing what the worst would be like, casually leafing through the countless written testimonials that one could find in the media at that time, not reading the whole article, because it was all a sorcerer's spell that would make those horrible things manifest, or I'd skim the testimonials to see the end, the worst, the ugliest, to get it over with. In Seattle, we carried on with hushed nerve. Cesar wasn't well enough established to leave Philip's basement, and he was such a good relief and company. The three of us would have long dinners when Cesar was off work; he had now learned how to cook marvelous food much in the same way he had learned to speak English, almost magically, out of thin air. Besides, his bossy manner suited him perfectly to be a chef. Of course, he had applied for work with a padded resumé that stated he had gone to a culinary school in New York, and armed with several letters of reference skillfully written by Philip himself, whose verbal silence always contrasted his flawless use of the written word.

ON HIS WAY IN AND OUT OF SEATTLE, CAMILO always stayed in Vancouver just long enough to get clean clothes, and books, and to pay his bills. He showed no attachment to his shoddy living quarters in Vancouver. It was a miracle that the place had not gone up in flames yet, as Mariana often turned the oven on to warm the place up, then would pass out drunk on the old hide-a-bed in the living room. When she was sober, or not high on weight loss pills, she spoke intensely about going back to Santiago with her new flame, a sleazy Chilean who fed liberal *gringos* the political refugee line and once in a blue moon worked as a performance artist, but lived off several welfare cheques he collected every month. One of the odd weekend evenings Camilo spent in Vancouver, Andrew took him out for dinner and partly amused, partly alarmed, told him that Mariana had gotten piss drunk at his place some evenings ago and had tried to get him into bed.

"I don't have any problem with women and sex, but I don't want to have sex with *her*."

Camilo inquired with great candor, "You have sex with women?"

"Well, of course, don't we all?" Andrew seemed concerned about a different matter. "It makes me wonder, you know, Garth and I are having a bit of a rough time – I don't mean to compare, I know what you must be – no, I can't imagine what you must be going through."

"I've never had sex with a woman!" Camilo confessed, and Andrew gave him a puzzled smile. And then, in a philosophical tone, he included, "You know, top, bottom – who the fuck cares. I'm a man, never wanted to be a woman, but I have always felt like a woman in bed." Camilo tried to disentangle the contradiction without hurting his friend. "Okay, I don't have a clue of how women feel, really, but all I know is that when I'm getting it on, I don't feel the way men are supposed to feel. It's hard to explain. Anyway, I thought bisexuality was now an unsafe sex crime or a passing trend for young homosex-ual kids – it's none of my business but . . . you and Sol? . . ."

"Yes." Andrew smiled sweetly, but he did not want to talk about the subject anymore.

"I respect that," Camilo said sincerely.

PHILIP STEADILY LOST WEIGHT AND ENERGY. WE became a bit more withdrawn from others – a mix of embarrassment, fear, and intolerance for the healthy – as we got terribly close to each other because the contact of our skins had become essential. At that time, we stopped engaging in sex with other men, which we had done every now and then. Cesar would come home from his new day job at a local airline to find us in silence. Chela's regular notes accented my gloomy days and I tried to reply, but for the most part, I didn't feel like writing at all. Philip arranged to go on early retirement from the job he had had for so many years. We made plans to go to Europe with his retirement money, but it was a banal dream. Springtime came and with it a bit of relief, there were news items about miraculous cures everywhere, and activists laying on the streets, getting their profiles drawn in chalk, telling people they would die if they were silenced. One day we found ourselves in the middle of an ACT UP demo down Broadway Avenue almost by chance, and there we ran into one of our sporadic third sexual parties; a Japanese skateboarder, young and earnest, who reminded me of *el gitano* in some ways. Philip and I made a quick comment that it was good to see some of our men still alive, not in denial, fighting for the politics of the plague.

In my many moments of guilt, I thought I had too many men, too much sex. At other times, I thought it was a sign of power and not a sign of moral decay. In any case, I accepted what life bestowed upon me. Philip wasn't well and having sex was a chore in those conditions – however, necessity being the mother of all inventions made him a powerful ringmaster and made me the heartfelt apprentice of randy choreographies carefully set up with occasional company. The grungy, stringy Japanese fellow we had met earlier and had reconnected with at the ACT UP demo became a regular guest. He would lean his skate-board against the wall outside the back door and swagger in with great panache, permanently plugged into a CD player that blared Nirvana, wearing dirty and loose army fatigues and a short t-shirt that generously regaled everyone with the sight of his firm, bare midriff and the crack of his lovely ass. His hair was always a mishmash of colours, his ears and his cock could not have sustained one more piercing. Understatedly, he had told us that he had been infected when messing with hard drugs, then he candidly explained that that was now in the past, that now he'd only do "crystal." After smoking a few joints or bumming Marinol pills that had been prescribed to Philip, we would play, the skateboarder stoically enduring all kinds of treatment of the flesh under Philip's absorbed gaze and his exact orders. What was surprisingly different for me was that Philip gradu-ally adjusted our scripts and actions so I'd end up playing the top to this kid and to others. Late at night, Philip would fall asleep, sitting in a big armchair by the door, breathing agitatedly; Socrates, the judi-cious cat, would pace the room quietly, and I'd put into practice on gagged, blindfolded, restrained men what I had learned. In the high-est points of these exorcisms, some guys would piss themselves, they'd moan like cubs or plead for mercy – if I hesitated and started to free them, they'd boldly refuse. Up to that point, I had always either tried to be appealing or appeasing to other men. Philip was passing a cer-tain wisdom and power on to me. It would eventually be my choice to lead my sexuality in a way I had never done before.

On one of those strange days, I jotted down the following thoughts to Chela: The border between Canada and the States is an oozing scar that never heals, the edge of an internment camp where our dreams are permanently quarantined. Canada, allegedly my country, is the golden cage, it represents material comfort, but it is not where my heart is. It is all about rational reasons to keep the sheer lunacy of this illness at bay. I have to maintain my residence in British Columbia to have the medical coverage, to finish my degree. Philip can't move to Canada because he would lose his health benefits package. It is a moot point by now, anyway. For the first time, some of that gay liberation bullshit makes sense. If only we were considered real human beings with real families of choice, we could choose what is really best for the two of us. I have tried to get a job in Seattle, but it is tough and I don't have any experience here. I am, again, a foreigner. Technically, I'm not even allowed to enter this country because I am infectious. Cesar has been a great companion – I know he is not *santo de tu devoción*, you think he's stuck up – and he spends several days at a time with us; now that he's training as a flight attendant, he'll start to fly soon, which is his lifelong dream. Who said that we would not all be queens?

ALTHOUGH CAMILO TRIED TO FIND SOLACE IN recording the daily events of that time, he rarely wrote to Chela or Ramiro. Andrew phoned often, as did Sol, but Camilo could not get involved in any meaningful exchange, his sentences were uncommonly succinct and unadorned. At the end of that summer Philip was so frail that he was not able to dig up his dahlia bulbs from the flowerbeds at Volunteer Park. His fellow members of the Puget Sound Dahlia Club finished the work for him. They were nice and helpful, straight folks who loved him for his love of flowers and his no-nonsense attitude, but were scared and did not come around often. Philip stayed inside almost all day, in front of the television. Camilo would sometimes force him to turn it off and play some of his favourite classical music or read to him out loud. The rest of their prolonged days, Philip helped Camilo to edit every page of his thesis; he methodically cut words and sentences much the same way he lovingly cut the buds off young dahlias growing downstairs under the hot lamps to make the stems stronger. At bedtime, Camilo would hold him in his arms and read him the scenes from his favourite cartoon book, *Calvin & Hobbes*, as Philip followed the pictures until he fell asleep.

I COULD VOMIT AND CONSUME SIMULTANEOUSLY with Philip. Every ounce of life I saw leaving his body, every bout of nausea and spew, also carried away a piece of my life. I struggled to keep my spirit buoyed above the surface of the uncontrollable gushes he expelled. If I had never seen a man eating shit out of pure lust, I would have never been able to face Philip's majestic bowel movements, his atrocious pain, and the perplexed look in his blue eyes. If I had never received the hands of men inside, I wouldn't have understood the borderline between pain and pleasure, between fear and desire. I wouldn't have been able to cope with consumption. If we had never played sexually with enemas – like primeval children playing with mud – the sight of such corporeal misery would have disgusted me. I wouldn't have had the courage to understand the imperfections of the body while everything around me insisted that bodies are forever young, athletic, immaculate, and vibrant. Doctors and nurses gave me their fucking *gringo* pep talk.

Cesar and I had to deal with Philip's family who started to come around for the first time. At first, these encounters had us all acting clumsily and uncomfortably. Every time they came, they stayed a bit longer, and squeezed as much as they could from me. They wanted to understand what it was like to be gay, to be infected, everything. Cesar – having gone through this ordeal with Juan – was protective and practical. He figured out what to do and did it without hesitation. He said that the jobs of nurses and flight attendants are alike, that they work for little money under catastrophic conditions, they have to be resolute and caring at the same time, while everyone around is being a pain in the ass. In one of our most confidential conversations, I told him how sorry I was I had all but ignored him all this time, though I was the one who had insisted that he move out here from New York. I was sorry he had to go through adversity like this once more in his life. As always he was on my side, no questions asked, no demands. Cesar also said that no matter how different he and Philip were, they had learned to respect and even love each other as roommates. Then Cesar gently made me deal with the reality of what would happen. "The first thing you must do is to make Philip sign all the necessary papers: will, insurance papers, powers of attorney, you name it," he said. "Las *cuentas claras conservan la amistad solía decir Juan – que en paz descanse la muy loca*. Philip is stunned, but he has to make some hard decisions now, otherwise you'll be at the mercy of his family – you've seen them; they might be sad and confused now but – believe me – people become vultures in situations like this – *aves de rapiña*."

Nothing can describe the sadness I felt that night, that one horrendous first night in which I had to get up and go and sleep on the couch in the living room. Sleeping embraced with Philip would never be possible again; his body, the rugged man that made me feel protected when he generously covered my body with his, had become an absurd stick figure. I had worked so hard to earn the right to share a bed with another man, free of guilt, openly, joyfully, and now this. I was furious at everything. At night, Philip would labouriously get up to come and get me to go back and lay next to him and hold his lovely head in my hands. I'd do this for a while, but it wasn't long before he would be sweating or vomiting. A few days later, I moved downstairs with Cesar. We slept by the empty dahlia hotbeds with a walkie-talkie next to our heads, activated by Philip's shrieks, coughs, and moans. Many times a night, we would take turns running upstairs to help him, often not sleeping at all. During the course of what became the longest autumn of my life – even longer than this one I face now – I never went back to Vancouver. Andrew and Sol dealt with Mariana, my rent, and even with my university paperwork and payments. Philip was in and out of the hospital several times. When he was there, I'd walk up Capitol Hill to the hospital every morning. The cold windy rain soothed me. On my way down, the Japanese skateboarder would zigzag between the street and the sidewalk and dodge the cars downhill for my amusement. Sometimes we'd grab a bite to eat, go home, eat, jack off, and fall asleep and I'd wake up in the middle of the night with an aching neck. He would be gone.

DURING THOSE LONG, DRAWN-OUT EVENINGS when Philip was sedated and his family had gone home for the day, Cesar and Camilo found a pastime: they would dress in drag and lip-synch to silly songs in the basement. *When you're alone and life is making you lonely /You can always go /Downtown /When you got worries /All the noise and the hurry seems to help /I know /Downtown.* They would laugh hard and sometimes run upstairs and perform a routine or two for Philip, who would wake up and watch in amazement. By then his smile had become a sardonic grin hanging like a hammock between a pair of jawbones. One evening, while Cesar and Camilo were trying on outfits and make-up in the basement while the Japanese skateboarder leaned against the wall with a lustful smile, smoking dope and casually fondling his cock, they heard Philip throwing up. In high heels, Cesar and Camilo ran upstairs, followed by the skateboarder, only to come face to face with Philip's father who had just walked in the door for the first time since Philip had become very ill. His jaw dropped at the sight of them, and then he coughed up a rusty hello. In high heels and clunky jewels Camilo and Cesar did what they were by then used to doing, carefully rolling Philip over, always talking in soft tones in his ear, all the while looking like well-seasoned yet deranged nurses, cleaning, changing the bed linen, and emptying the drainage bag. Philip's father muttered a good-night and walked out of the room. On his way out, he almost broke his skull when he tripped on the Japanese fellow's skateboard. Once he was gone, they all, even Philip, had a good laugh. *You can forget all your troubles /Forget all your cares /And you may find somebody kind /To help and understand you /Someone who is just like you /And needs a gentle hand to guide them along.*

Philip passed away peacefully at the end of October. His last breath was deep and rusty like an old machine that breaks down. No one saw the small pilgrimage of shadows that silently left the house before the first break of early morning light: the ugly Trotskyite and Camilo's family doctor who had come from Vancouver, the Japanese skateboarder, Cesar who had to work a morning flight to New York, and a lanky fellow from the Hemlock Society chapter in Seattle. Camilo and Socrates, the judicious cat, sat vacantly for three hours until the morning light fully invaded every corner of the house. There were bright flowers in big vases, light curtains, and soft classical music playing; the last time Philip had been admitted to the hospital for a couple of days, Camilo, Cesar, and the Japanese fellow had painted the room in a lovely, soft sepia colour. After a while, Camilo made a few phone calls to doctors and family, speaking calmly and self-assuredly. He only provided the necessary information — maybe the IV machine had stopped a while that night or maybe the increased doses of morphine in the last two days had something to do with it. His family suggested that Philip could have lasted longer if he had been interned permanently in a care facility; they spoke in concerned and muffled tones, as if they were speaking about a defective toy whose date of expiration had not come.

I NEVER ADMITTED TO ANYTHING EXCEPT THAT I was glad to see Philip go; whatever push we gave him, I know his soul needed it to escape his unsteady prison of flesh wounds and bones. I felt an intense relief then – no more shit, no more vomit, no more pain, no more morphine-induced delusions, and no more squeals. I saw his energy being released into the air above the bed, hovering above the house on Olive Way, above Capitol hill, above Seattle, above Washington State, and then disappearing. It wasn't angelical or spiritual, it was the energy of a man on death row, once jailed, now free. Whatever their real feelings towards us, Philip's family came that morning to seek comfort. I wondered what was wrong with that picture, but then, when Philip's dad broke down, and his wife and children stood there petrified, unable to do anything, I felt I had to find the right words to console them. None of them could bring themselves to do or say anything. At long last, they left crying, after telling us that no loss was as great as theirs. Two days after Philip's death, after the body had been taken to a funeral home, his mother and sisters were possessed by a fastidious need to make arrangements for a memorial that was to take place in a week, making plans as if they were preparing Rosemary's baby shower. They called insistently to check about the details – if we wanted to say something at the ceremony, about the flowers, the music he liked, the list of attendants, and to ask us to find tokens and old photos among Philip's household clutter. In the end, we didn't go to the memorial. I couldn't participate in a situation where Cesar and I would not be treated as family. I wanted to be treated with the pomp and respect provided to widows, but I knew there was no way I'd get that. I did not consider standing quietly at a funeral for the sake of others. I knew it would be a sanitized occasion where his memory would be stripped of his strong and sexual body, his urges and exploits, and his fine sense of irony.

Nothing bad comes in one single blow – *nos llovió sobre mojado*. Exactly a week after Philip's cremation, the apartment superintendent, who had known Philip for the fifteen years he had rented his place, knocked at the door and told us point blank that we had to vacate at the end of the month. In a tiny, whiny voice, he said that he had mentioned to us the renewal of the lease and we had done nothing about it. Cesar was outraged and punched him in the face. Holding his bleeding nose, the super threatened to call the police and scurried away like a rat through the courtyard. At the end of the following month, in terrible weather, Cesar moved to a new place on Aurora Street and took Socrates with him. I packed up Philip's apartment and executed his will – much to the chagrin of his family he had left everything he owned to me, and had signed his life insurance over to me. Andrew came to Seattle with a truck and drove me back to Vancouver. The day we emptied Philip's apartment, a strange emotion came over all of us and we kicked the walls in and spat on the floor in a frenzy of rage over the apartment, over Philip's death, over everything. That was the last time I saw the Japanese skateboarder, his knuckles bloody from so much hacking and pounding. Before he went on his way, he kissed me hard on the lips, his breath thick with dope smoke. Soon after coming back to Vancouver, my body erupted in a thousand places and I ended up in an emergency room. I couldn't breathe. I couldn't move. A few weeks later, I would defend my Master's degree at the university, mechanically, aided by friends and a very compassionate supervisor. None of that had any rhyme or reason any longer.

The Pacific Northwest and its vast spaces can at once be desolate and comforting for its inhabiting souls. I kept visiting Cesar in Seattle, driving recklessly across the Cascades – I was never a good driver and certainly the school where I bought my license wasn't a good one either – stopping at rest areas in the evenings to get on my knees and take delivery of the fluids of burly truckers who chew tobacco and spit in your eye. In Seattle, I spent endless nights at the same bathhouse where I had first met Philip, rabid on crystal and weed, unable to keep Philip's daunted figure away from my feverish mind, holding on to glimpses of anonymous torsos, fingers, lips, eyes, patches of hair, nails, loose body parts – *And solitaire is the only game in town/and every road that takes him, takes him down/and by himself it's easy to pretend/he'll never love again.* Of all the people in the world, I never expected to meet Sonny the jazz singer there, one night, covered with a small, frayed white towel, exposed under the glare of a dirty naked bulb. It was hard to recognize him at first, as he was very thin and his big white teeth were magnified in the interior twilight, appearing about to jump out of his mouth. His apparition terrified me, and when he came to touch me, I made up a stupid excuse that he could easily recognize as a lie, and stormed out of the bathhouse. That night, and countless others, I cruised the damp streets for hours. I'd pick up a mickey of gin, sit on the cold pavement, smoke, and eventually get picked up by some weirdo in a beat-up truck – I'd only go with the tough-looking ones – who would take me to some place and make me numb. I needed to learn to hate Seattle. I needed to escape. In my last lonely nights there I could only amble, seeing really emaciated men who looked like Karen Carpenter, singing low – *And keeping to himself he plays the game/without her love, it always ends the same/while life goes on around and everywhere, he's playing solitaire.*

Bent souls, twisted like corkscrews, can be found in the most wholesome of suburbs, in the healthiest of rural places. Deep in the restrained anxiety of the Northwest's eternal winters, entrenched in portables planted in the middle of large tracts of land, in overcrowded trailer parks, forty minutes from the closest convenience store, one can find a world of desperados infected by loneliness. I always thought that North American poverty strikes the soul, so different it is, in my view, from the material poverty I have seen in other places. It was uncanny how I could touch the lives of many and how I was touched by them. In roundabout ways I was touched by men made quirky by the desolation in their lives, working odd jobs, smoking dope late into the night, doing hard drugs, and drinking stale beer. However, something was slowly but surely changing within me. Although I craved the company of men like one struggles for breath, I began to resist being forced on my knees. I didn't want to be drenched in fluids anymore. I didn't want to be handled and discarded. Something like a religious atonement stung me inside every time a transient stranger came my way – and I was getting to meet lots of them. I had dough to get us drugs and booze – and I would show them a good time, and I would show them how to let go. By way of this jarring method of liberation, I began to make tough guys suffer the bristle of my close-cropped head, my cold lips wet with acidic saliva, sinking my teeth into nipples and buttocks. Some would say that misery loves company, but I found out that those harsh men know how to appreciate a person who has decided to leave all of the conventional bullshit of the world behind. Jesus Christ told the disciples to stop throwing their nets to catch fish and start fishing for men. I got the right lines, the right turns of phrase. I turned to gaybashers, alcoholics, bikers with branded torsos, carpet-baggers, sawmill workers who had been laid off and went from town to town trying to make ends meet, angry white teenagers who rightly thought their world was shit, unemployed white trash, rednecks, sulky Chicano men with hands calloused from picking and squeezing ripe fruit for meagre salaries. I turned to all kinds of men who were skittish, disrespected, and despised, and they put their lives into my hands – who would have thought? The last thing these men wanted was a fucking *spic* to wring deep-rooted and sinister desires out of them – I had learned my ways. I absorbed their frustration with every pore of my skin. I made them turn the other cheek and then I kicked it with a heavy steel-toed boot. Then I recited a twisted line into their ears, pushed reality up their noses, stuffed it in their every orifice – "See what life does to you, every day? – Fucks you up," I told them while riding and straddling, sensing the fine tissue tearing inside, and hearing a mantra in the abandon of their moans. "Feel the humiliation? Yeah, you do? It's like poison, man, ain't it? It's like an inoculation – you know what that means, right? Only by taking it in, you can see your own failure, buddy. Only by getting it you can find a cure." I conquered the men who were duly impressed by a blown-up operetta of abject despair. I got them doused in alcohol and banged them hard on scratched pool tables, after the last bar call, after the roaring Harley engines had died at the back door, "Take me raw, buddy. Now you know what fucks you up, boy, now you can fight it." I took them face down in the mossy mud of the humid forests, and in the last pew of churches that only opened for business on weekends. "Yeah, right, buddy, it's a dog-eat-dog world, better fuck them before they fuck you, take me up, buddy, take me raw!" There were gasps, convulsions, screams, incredible ejaculations and, after a while, a silence and a gaping blackout.

In those days, I disappeared from Vancouver for weeks at a time, didn't return any of the concerned calls I received, didn't even know what Mariana was doing or what was going on with my place or any of my material possessions. However, I never stopped writing, in those few moments of rest, in dingy motels along the west coast trails, in Port Alberni, Dawson Creek, Portland, Eureka, in the always agitated and crisply turned-out San Francisco, in the mellow Pismo Beach of San Luis Obispo, like a holy roller, I sat in the faint morning light, and while smoking one cigarette after the other I carefully composed my prayers in letters to my mother, Chela, Ramiro in London, to Leandro, and even one to the *gitano* – little did I know that he had passed away. In one of those letters, I confessed to Leandro that I knew I was infected when we fucked in *La Habana*. I didn't do this out of remorse. I wrote that nothing one does in the name of love is ill-conceived, it's just plain stupid. I wrote that letter because I felt untidy; I needed to clear the bits and pieces from my head. I didn't implore his forgiveness, I asked him to go and find out whether he was infected or not. I wouldn't plead for things I hadn't done alone – no more Catholic bullshit – but I knew he had to take care of himself. In impeccable calligraphy, I wrote one page after the other, bleeding words and understanding, the way one preaches the word. I wrote my mother a long letter in which I told her Philip had died peacefully and that I was taking some time to see what I would do. I told her nothing she didn't know before, but I said things that needed to be spelled out. I enclosed a cheque with some of the cash Philip had left me so she could finish buying her house, our first home, which we would never inhabit together. I told her it was possible that we'd never be close again but that we'd never really be apart either. I told her I was truly okay in Canada – I really was, because frenzied as I was, I had at last come into my own. I told my mother I understood why she had sacrificed so much of her own life, working year in and year out, a modern slave, with two afternoons free a week, so I could have a good life. I said thank you.

We men have a weird way of showing loyalty when we temporarily satisfy each other, our needs overflowing without saying a word. We seem willing to give up our soul without explanation to cults or strangers, as long as we do not know, as long as we don't have to face the reality with those who truly love us. We turn fanatical, religious, become junkies, serial killers, or pedophiles. I met so many men in those days who were escaping from their moment of truth or from the boring reality of their lives. I preferred the down-and-out ones, the guys who had been left out, who had never got what they say we can buy on television – success, health, and youth – men who had only looked at each other with suspicion and seen the Chinese, the Mexican, or the Polish – always a stranger – move to the good land, the gentrified neighbourhood, to displace them, who were denied welfare, who were denied what they had been brought up to believe was rightfully owed to them by society. They genuflected, their faces enshrined in my ass, my hands landing like heavy birds on their bare skin, my words burning their ears, humiliating, making them break down, only to hold them up at the last possible moment while crying in my arms. Only then I told them that I loved them. They dwelled in despair, in the thickness of my seed, the stench of their own feces and musty urine. I wolfed them down, chewed them through the convulsive nights to ultimately spew them into the early morning to die their small deaths.

Springtime in Vancouver surprised me with an exotic bouquet of purple flowers on my arms, a bunch of wild flowers I had gradually picked up from the roadside in my recent trips up and down the west coast. It didn't hurt at first, it only felt weird – I mean, my turning into the nightmare that everyone, every book, every safe sex brochure had promised me – it was surprising. Slowly, the purple flowers of my desire crept down my legs like poison ivy. I had only seen my body like this when I was living with Gabriel or Roger. This time, the purple blossoms of this macabre bridal wreath would not go away.

INITIALLY, CAMILO'S TERROR OF BEING REPUDIATED turned into a form of aggression, and then it quieted down into leniency towards the awkwardness of others. He stopped waiting on other people's feelings. Only a few of Camilo's closer friends such as Andrew, Cesar, and Sol learned to accept Camilo's ebbs and flows without censure.

"You know, Andrew, we should have been lovers," Camilo blurted out one day *apropos* of nothing.

Andrew, who had gained a refreshing serenity after he had shut Garth out of his life, smiled and responded, "I was trying to figure some things out then – like I am now."

"But that afternoon with you, it would have been glorious if you and I had had a go at it alone – but Garth was watching us."

"I agree. I did fancy your perky little *Latino* ass many times – that is, before you turned into the leather-clad bitch you are now."

"Hey, watch it, or I'll vomit on you." They laughed. Then they stopped, almost embarrassed to be disturbing the men in the other three beds in the ward.

Andrew mused about that evening long ago. "I also wanted to be respectful of Sol. She has always been there for me – for us." And he leaned over to Camilo and very gently kissed his dry lips.

Camilo was learning to employ the novel reactions he provoked in those around him and to speak his mind with a candor that startled some people. Shortly after that conversation with Andrew, in one of his frequent visits to his doctor, Camilo took the chance to raise a subject they had never discussed before.

"Hey, Doc, who are we fooling here? Take a good long at me, I'm getting covered in this shit." Camilo spoke casually as if discussing the weather. "Shit, don't you think we're doing it out of habit and duty? – We've had a good run, but. . . ."

"I'd be in great trouble if anybody ever knew about this and about. . . ." The doctor was a thick man in his fifties, one of those men who, no matter how hard they try, do not look homosexual and cannot behave as such.

"No worries, Doc, my lips are sealed – if you only knew the shit *I* know. Anyway, I don't seem to enjoy getting your anal probe as much as I used to, even my medical needs are changing." Coyly, Camilo let out a laugh and settled a hand on the doctor's shoulder. "And about Philip, Seattle and all that, I've already declared myself in deep dementia and incompetent." The doctor sighed and smiled lukewarmly.

Camilo painstakingly put his boxer shorts and t-shirt back on. "I'm no one to advise – see what my wisdom has done for me lately? – but, if I were you, I'd find myself a young boy – I mean, you're such a dutiful man, but you've got to get something going, for later."

The doctor laughed shyly. "I'm too old for that."

"Bullshit. There are plenty of young guys out there who want the status of having a doctor under their belt – not to mention the cash – and they'll put out gladly. Don't look at me like I'm the fucking Antichrist, for God's sake! You should've taken *me* up while I was with Roger. I was seeing you often – yeah, anal warts, remember? Pesky little plague that is – I would've done good by you. Instead you see what happened with Roger – what a fuck-up."

The doctor looked at Camilo with a mix of apprehension and patience. A few minutes later, he gently pushed him out the door and greeted his next client.

I DECIDED TO KICK MARIANA OUT THE DAY THAT Cesar phoned me with the news that Italo had passed away on the flight to Santiago – first class, of course. The bitch had borrowed money to fly to New York and be by Italo's side in what she called his "moment of worst affliction" and she had taken off, who knows where, with her latest squeeze, an esoteric young East Indian man who wanted to realign her chakras by applying his counterfeit version of the Kama Sutra, which – of course – required illicit substances and shitloads of money. She never cleaned, cooked, or paid rent – needless to say, she was never sober enough to offer any help when they started me on chemotherapy and radiation and I came back home in excruciating pain. That same day I got Leandro's letter in the mail saying that he was not positive – thanks to the missionary positions and the hetero roles, that had something to do with it – and the letter said that although he knew I'd never come back, he would always love me, and there was no forgiveness because there was no harm or sin done. He appended his writing by telling me that he had never had another man after me, and that he would never have another one, ever. His woman and his children were doing fine and had happily accepted the presents they had received from a stranger in Canada. He never again mentioned his wanting to leave behind *la familia*, his old abode in *La Habana Vieja* or *la revolución*. It was with glee that as soon as Mariana showed up later that week, I threw her belongings out the window.

AT LAST, AT THE END OF AN EXCEPTIONALLY DRY summer, a call from Chela came to break Camilo's solitude in the hospital room. He had been in and out of the hospital often that season. That day Camilo was in good spirits and they exchanged niceties; oddly, hearing each other's voices was strange, they were used to reading each other's thoughts in long letters.

"She is desolate, the poor thing, she feels you were harsh with her." Chela had called at Mariana's request to try to make amends for what had happened.

Camilo's voice curved into sarcasm. "Yeah, poor thing." And, after a pause, Camilo changed the subject for the second time. "So, what's up with you?"

"Not much, darling. A young man is shooting an experimental documentary about my life – he's the cutest boy, from the film department at the university Uli attends."

"I thought Uli would be a lawyer by now."

"He is. This is graduate work, *amorosa*."

"I see – anyway, a nurse is here writing about my life – Kirsten, the woman I traveled with to Cuba."

Chela's tone changed slightly. "Oh, I see. What are you telling her?" Then her tone turned a notch more defensive. "You're *not* letting her read our letters, right?" And there was a transcontinental moment of silence. "I trust you, I mean, there are things that one must keep secret."

Camilo shifted his legs in the bed, uncomfortable. "If you tell at least one person, it is not a secret anymore."

"Camilo, cut the crap. What are you trying to say?"

"You never had any problem telling everyone that I was infected."

"Please, *bonita*, you did it yourself, your body was fairly . . . public in this town, wasn't it?" Chela's lukewarm gag had a trace of accusation in it.

Camilo's voice broke down due to lack of oxygen and a touch of irritation. "Is this what it is all about? My fucking? Me having a good time and your not getting it on?" He inhaled with difficulty to add, "If me telling anyone that you were never infected is your fear, don't you worry, *darling*, I won't."

"Okay, okay, I get it, you might be a bit – let's say, a bit envious 'cause you never got to do the things I've done here as an immigrant."

"Ha! Spare me! Envious? Fuck that! 'Cause I didn't build an operation around a fucking lie? You must be joking. And, what *immigrant* are you talking about? You and I know full well there was never a *gringa*, that's another lie. You didn't have the balls to go back to Chile the way you *really* were, accept who you really *are* –"

"Shut the fuck up! You said we'd never discuss this."

"You brought it up – accusing me of being envious, the nerve!" Camilo had a brief coughing fit.

"Admit it, darling." Chela seemed to have regained some of her usual sangfroid. "I have made it and *that* makes many people jealous. Not you in particular."

"Don't you get it? I'm not jealous of a lie. I'm not jealous of having to tell a young trophy boyfriend that I'm positive to trip him on pity and guilt for years, even if he didn't touch me with a nine-inch pole."

"You can be a cruel and vindictive bitch when you have nothing to lose." Chela's voice dripped with scorn, but this did not stop Camilo.

"I'm losing my fucking life here and still you're green that I fucked my jolly way through it. I had the youth and the energy to do it." Camilo delivered his indictment with clarity. "You keep a lie that makes you a queen, but an aging and untouchable queen."

"Me? Envious of what? That you decided to commit suicide by splitting your body apart bit by bit with tweezers and whips, that you've infected everything that crosses your way – you must be mental!" Chela was livid. She had lost her cool and Camilo was not listening anymore, a nurse had come, replacing the oxygen mask on his mouth, and softly taking the phone away from him. She hurriedly said a few words of explanation to Chela and hung up.

MY LESIONS ARE ANGRY. I USED TO STAY QUIET waiting for the heavy opiate sheath of morphine to muffle my pain, but now it never ceases, and is more intense than any sex I ever had. It fucks me hard, it keeps on fucking until it is not fun anymore and when I want it to stop, it doesn't, and I realize I'm not at a party any more. I sink my teeth into my hand and howl inside. I flinch, jolt, and wail like a wild animal under siege, before the other pain starts again. It took me a lifetime to understand my body, to feel comfortable with who I am, with its virtues and blemishes, and where I am located in the world, but now I have to let go of it, the flesh that gave me so much pleasure, the centre of so many sensations. I wish I could inflict this pain on others, so they would know, so they would swallow their platitudes like I swallow my shrieks. For hours at a time I go crazy, *loca zafada*, cracked, *loca de casa de orates*, lunatic. Startled, I wake up several times each night, *nadie duerme a mi lado*, no seaport in sight, only a detached hand, *una voz dulce pero sin labios*, an instrument of torture, another inoculation, *otra lanza a mi costado*, someone punctures Santa Sebastiana, someone forces Marilyn to swallow those pills, someone injects Billie with heroin, *y me atraviesan con esos rayos invisibles e inodoros*, someone lights the fire under *Juanita de Arco*, someone gives Judy another drink, someone steals Evita's embalmed body, someone sees a deranged *La Lupe* disappear in the streets of a big city, someone officiously reads the life signs, a grooved line, someone upsets the flat line, the steady straight line I have been wishing for. *Las aguas turbias lo envenenan todo y necesito escapar por las alcantarillas hasta desembocar en el mar limpio.* I let the morphine lick me up with its giant tongue of elation like I let men hang their tongues out like dogs to lick my ass.

The psychedelic diorama of ghosts makes me nauseous and I can't contain the torrent of bodily fluids. My body fails me after carrying me over grand epics, now my everyday life is reduced to cryptic notes jotted down in a journal by Kirsten, once again my accidental travel companion. What a providential encounter, she understands me, I think, I trust her – at least she understands when I speak in tongues. Then, the show must go on, sometimes I am a character in one of those strange productions at *El Goce Pagano*. A gorgeous straight boy who looks like Uli but Caucasian, who will earnestly devote his privileged life to help his fellow men, holds my hand without flinching – a doctor without borders – and he looks at me as if he understands. A troupe of wannabe medics often circles me in mid-morning, I think they will break into a song, one of those musical numbers that Philip liked so much, or a dissonant torch ballad that Chela likes to lip-synch to, they are like the dreadful gay men's choirs that exist in each city, a garland of earnest mouths always sounding out a perfectly round "o." They must concentrate on doing that by imagining they have a huge cock to suck on – I see them clearly now, they are like a school of devilish penguins, gathered around me with demure attitudes. They talk to each other, nod, poke, assent – they must suffer from Tourette's syndrome – finally someone, the instructor, directs a couple of obligatory statements to me and they all leave.

Philip, my dear Philip, you who are up above, look at me – *Padre nuestro que estas en los cielos, santificado sea tu nombre. . . .* If only I had turned into a lacto-ovo vegetarian freak I'd be in shape. *Por mi culpa, por mi culpa, por mi gran culpa. . . .* If I had avoided hypertension, cholesterol, cellulite, depression, alcoholism, unsafe fucking, exploitative work hours, and bad one-night-stands. *No nos dejes caer en la tentación y libranos de todo mal ahora y en la hora de nuestra muerte. . . .* If I had gulped down all my little pills on time. *Angel de la guarda, dulce compañia, no me desampares ni de noche ni de dia. . . .* If I had avoided operatic scenes of love and sex . . . *santificado sea tu reino, hagase tu voluntad tanto en la tierra como en los cielos.* . . . If I had followed all the guidelines, rules, policies, and instructions these *gringos* have created so that they can regulate every fucking minute of our fucking anal retentive lives, I could have survived. I have packed too much into these years. I'm overloaded with grudges, hatred, mistakes, desires, recantations . . . *perdona nuestros pecados así como nosotros perdonamos a los que nos ofenden.* . . . Now, I have to cleanse, I don't want my soul stuck in traffic purgatory.

 CESAR VISITS AS OFTEN AS HIS WORK SCHEDULE
in Seattle permits, and each time he brings ice
cream to soothe Camilo's throat carpeted in white
candida. Dressed in his impeccable flight attendant
uniform, he regales Camilo with stories about
flights and planes that travel far away as he patiently spoons the ice cream through his chapped lips.
Unfortunately, and unexpectedly, Sol and Andrew
have moved to Dawson Creek. Sol used to sit next
to Camilo in the evenings and tell him about her
ideas for new movie scripts, about her son, and her
friendship with Andrew. Now, they sweetly try to
shorten the distance by calling often. One day she and Andrew timidly break the news to Camilo – they are in love, and they are getting
married. Andrew picks up the phone after Sol, the time seems to stop,
and Camilo and Andrew fall back into those cozy days in which they
told each other everything about their lives.

"For so many years I lived for Garth." Andrew paused and
Camilo sighed on the other end of the phone line. "Now I see how
I treated Garth as a wife, I adored him as a woman, I fucked him as a
woman – all the *gay* things I did, I did for him, not for me."

Camilo spoke slowly. "I understand. Believe me, I do, even
when you say that 'homosexuality is unnatural,' I know how you
mean it."

"You do?" Andrew sounds reassured and relieved. "I know it is an
odd thing to say – or do – but I truly saw it when Garth dumped me
and I went on that sex rampage. I was crazed, I was erratic. I understand
why you've done what you have done, the sex is good, the sex is okay
– I mean, the leather thing, the hunger . . . but love, that kind of love
between two men, it's unnatural, not because it's bad, but it's so
impossible – it's so fucking impossible to. . . ."

"Sustain."

"Yeah, it's too intense, too demanding . . . fuck! They've turned it into an impossible standard. I mean it has less and less to do with feelings, yours and mine . . . this is hard to explain, this is where I am at – need I tell you of the times I have been accused of betrayal, homophobia, and going back into the closet?"

"What has always mattered is our love, and who we are." And Camilo lets go of that topic to relate to Andrew Mariana's latest exploits, that she has never come to visit but sometimes phones. "She slurs her words, she says that she and her latest fling, a fifty-year-old hippie, are going to California to join some cult, study James Redfield's texts, and chant for the realignment of my body, soul, and destiny." Camilo's breathing is agitated, but he manages to keep his train of thought. "In the same breath, she talked about going back to Chile to repossess *El Goce Pagano*. I told her she was a freak." Andrew laughs and they talk quietly on the phone a while longer, speaking in tongues.

A QUIET STORM THRUSTS MY BODY AGAINST THE wall with silent fury. A shroud of dusky clouds hurries over the limpid sky. From this window, I can't see English Bay and the east side of Vancouver which I miss so much. I can't see Seattle, Santiago, or *La Habana*. I see how the others carry on with their lives wearing their sensitive skins that can register seismic desires and pleasures. My skin feels like parchment, mute and insensitive. I peek out my hospital door, I see the healthy men, orderlies, and hospital cleaners. I see the bulk underneath the blue cotton. How dead must one be to forget all about sex and concentrate on the fucking spirit, I wonder. They think that dying people don't feel or notice. They come and knock at the door – come out and play, they say, my ghosts that is – come and do the cha-cha, come and skip rays of sun. I choose to stay behind the door, clandestine, like the son of a servant in the kitchen, hoping that one day soon they'll get tired of trying to lure me out there. *Los chispazos de locura y lucidez que incendian el tramado hirsuto de mi mente afiebrada.* The morphine flows through my arteries carrying a thick syrup of visions. A beehive of puzzled eyes observes me from a distance, attentive to the tedious minutiae of my flimsy life signals. I wanted to be in my house surrounded by the objects I cherish with some of the people I love around me. I wanted to be with my lover. I tried this so hard and for so long. Now, I have nothing. My mind wanders in long corridors with a bouquet of purple flowers in my arms, wearing no slippers, and the cold, melancholic tiles refresh my fiery feet.

I heard that Roger died last weekend, or maybe the weekend before that. What envy I felt, that even in the end he got to go first, to have his way. During that very hard period of time before I met Philip, every time I thought I was over Roger, he'd come unannounced, late in the evening when Mariana was too drunk to pay attention to anything. He would trample into the apartment looking agitated and before I could react he had closed the blinds, turned the lights off, and turned the stereo on. His tongue would always choke the words in my throat, his tongue would force me on my knees, his tongue would make me roll over and play dead. Like the most stereotypical queen – *la loca* – born to be loved and punished by her man, I didn't resist his onslaught while making believe that he would take me back, and making mental promises to myself that this would be the last time. He would choke me until I blacked out, and inside that darkness, I could see an implosion of small bright lights. We'd both wake up drenched in bitter sweat and silence. Then he would throw a couple of bills at me and leave me staring at the cockroaches crawling through the carpet at the edge of the room, crying quietly.

In those wee hours of the morning I think about the afterlife – *los recuerdos se entrecruzan, surcen y cauterizan en mi mente para conjurar tu rostro Leandro, la gente blanca entra a esta blanca habitación sin hacer ruido y me clavan sus instrumentos a quemarropa, las uñitas afiladas de palomas tétricas. . . .* When I'm gone, when I'm nothing, even less than a speck of dust, I want my body cremated at infernal temperatures to do away with viruses, bacteria, spirochetes, amoebas, and the sinister wreaths of purple flowers that envelope my cadaver *quiero consumirme en un fuego eterno como el ardor y el celo de los hombres.* Keep my ashes to be mixed with those of Philip in a beautiful wooden box where purple dahlias should be planted and cared for until they grow and bloom – *hasta que la muerte nos separe, porque el sufrió y murió en la cruz, en esta cama de hospital, para la salvación de las almas de todos los embusteros, los promiscuos, los groseros, los celosos, los buenos y santos hombres* – and I don't want an obituary to appear in print with a cheap black and white photo in which I'm smiling contritely. If a eulogy needs to be written for the sake of protocol, which I adore, I want it to be written in Spanish and

English – *murió como la Santa Sebastiana que era, cruzada por las sondas clínicas, los destellos de cromo, y la anestesia de la vida que se escapa de la verga de un gran hombre* – I want the writing to make my friends cry because it is cleansing, let them cry, bastards, let them cry, sisters, *Todas íbamos a ser reinas / y de verídico reinar / pero ninguna ha sido reina / ni en Arauco ni en Copán.* . . . Someone should collect what I have written over the years, letters, stories, poems, shopping lists, to-do lists, threatening notes, yellow post-its, layers of skin, all of it flammable.

Borders are like oozing wounds, they never heal – *aunque tu te entreges y yo me entrege a ti, al placer de las palabras hilvanadas con deseo, habrá siempre una vida que nos desarraige a jirones* – a few words to stitch the time together, to keep it seamless – *pero todo instrumento es inútil para cauterizar esta herida púrpura, esta profundidad, y esta lejanía* – to measure the depth of my life, place your finger in my wound and tell me how deep you can go. Seeing is believing – now, switch me off, turn the page – you promised – *y ahora cumple tu palabra, y que la morfina, química amiga, recia y tibia, me sostenga en la travesía con su músculo fuerte* – at the end of the day there is always one more man to save the day and not write it off as a bad journey. *Leandro, ya pasó la época del cha-chachá y solo veo un mar en calma que se extiende ante nosotros, y su lengua delicada nos recoge, nos lleva, nos mece, nos despoja de todo lo innecesario, y desnudos nos deposita en la orilla una vez más con un suspiro de espuma blanca.* I see Philip, holding his loving dominion, sitting on a throne amidst a field of purple dahlias that wave to the whistle of a gentle breeze – *el océano de flores se despereza, y con un gesto tierno nos vuelve a bautizar enteros* – somewhere, someone whispers *"On the earth we will be queens / and we shall truly reign / and our kingdoms will be so vast / we will all reach the sea."* A sea of quietude comes and laps me up and draws me in, laps me up and deposits me back on the shore.